The Redneck Chronicles

3/11/04

The Redneck Chronicles

Brent Basham

iUniverse, Inc.
New York Lincoln Shanghai

The Redneck Chronicles

iUniverse, Inc.

For information address:
iUniverse, Inc.
2021 Pine Lake Road, Suite 100
Lincoln, NE 68512
www.iuniverse.com

ISBN: 0-595-30899-6

Printed in the United States of America

Contents

Acknowledgements

I'd like to take this time to thank my redneck family. Without each of you, none of this would have been possible. So, my deep gratitude goes out to (in no particular order): Mom, Dad, Kevin, Jeff, Shannon, John, Matt, Ruth, Mike, Jean, Corby, Sam, Pop, Granny Snookie, Grandma Joy, Karl, Elbert, Chris, Bonnie, Christian, Heather, Jacob, Michelle, Neal, Marcia, Bill, Cherie, Paul, Beverly, Karen, Tammy, Cleo, Alan, Beulah, Earl, Jimmy, Mike, and many other distant and extended relatives. Thanks for being you.

Introduction

What exactly *is* a redneck? What unique qualities must a person possess, to fit this widespread cultural phenomenon? You know, I have often wondered the very same thing myself. How does an individual earn such a dubious distinction? More than likely, merely mentioning the word brings strong visual images to your mind's eye. Perhaps you envision an unkempt middle-aged man, parked comfortably on his beat-up old sofa, searching violently through the clutter of empty beer cans for the television remote control. Or maybe you picture a single young mother instead, living on government provided welfare checks and chasing a houseful of children around the trailer.

We're probably all familiar with the more common stereotypes, often depicted in hit movies like *Joe Dirt* (David Spade) and *Vegas Vacation* (Randy Quaid). But if we are to gain a better understanding of these unique creatures, we must be willing to dig deeper, below the surface and into the heart of their lives. To do that properly we will need to enlist the help of a volunteer. Someone who's life might serve as a kind of historical case study, allowing us to reconsider many of our inaccurate and often outdated misconceptions. The question is, with such a negative connotation surrounding the word *redneck*, how could we ever find someone actually willing to admit to being one? What kind of person would let their life be placed under the microscope, every detail scrutinized just so we could satisfy our sense of curiosity?

I'm going to let you in on a little secret. I am a redneck. It has taken me a very long time, and many years of intensive therapy, to finally accept this simple fact. As a result the better part of my life has been spent in denial. There was no way I wanted to believe it was true. The signs were all there, but I refused to accept the inevitable. But you can't hide something like that forever. Sooner or later it was bound to come out. Looking back over my life it has become obvious that no matter how much I may have tried to ignore them, my redneck roots were here to stay.

Like the time I tied one end of a rope around a pecan tree behind our house and the other end around my waist playing Tarzan. I climbed to the highest point I could reach, tied one end off as securely as possible and leapt fearlessly into midair. My poor mother must've had a heart attack when she found me screaming at the top of my lungs, dangling from the branch of that tree. From the back porch there was no way she could've seen that the rope was tied around my waist, not my neck, so you can imagine how terrified she must've been. To this day, I still don't think she's quite forgiven me for the torture I put her through in my youth.

Or how about the fact that my younger brother Kevin now has a fake front tooth, courtesy of my cousin John and what has now become a notorious BB gun fight. It seems they were positioned directly across the yard from each other when John took aim at Kevin shooting him square in the mouth. He blacked out immediately from both the shock of being hit and the excruciating pain. Kevin wasn't completely blameless though, since they *both* had guns and they were *both* shooting at each other. Maybe he should be a little more careful about who he chooses to trade rounds with next time. As it turns out, John's quite the marksman (this wasn't the only live target he'd ever hit) and he's now put his skills to good use as a police officer in the United States Air Force. Up until a few years ago, my mother was still under the false impression that Kevin accidentally dropped the gun on the ground, causing it to go off and shoot him in the face. What a family.

I spent the formative years of my life, including much of my adolescence, in a small town called Lake City situated in the northern part of Florida. That may not immediately strike you as being redneck country but let me assure you, it more than qualifies. It's so close to Georgia that you could almost spit across the state line. As for the name, there are at least five lakes lying in close proximity to town. They have incredibly unique names too like Hamburger Lake (named for its round shape), Big Lake (you guessed it, the biggest lake in town), Alligator Lake (lots of gators), etc., and I am proud to say that I have personally fished in each and every one of them.

The picture you see on the front cover depicts Lake DeSoto, a small lake located right near downtown Lake City. They had just drained it for some reason so my dad decided to take Kevin and me fishing, redneck style. A photographer from the local newspaper was covering the event when our unusual behavior caught his attention. The sight of us struck him as being so funny that he just couldn't resist the chance to snap a few shots. There we were, two of the biggest rednecks in town, forever frozen in time by this guy's handiwork.

That's me in the cover photo, taking time out to counsel with Kevin (in the Harley Davidson jeans jacket) about our strategy of catching fish without the benefit of a fishing pole. Apparently due to a decreased amount of oxygen in the water, the fish were moving much slower than usual. Slow enough in fact that we were able to catch them with nothing but our bare hands. As you might've noticed from the picture, Kevin is much dirtier than I am and his no-holds-barred, aggressive style of fishing turned out to be extremely productive. He caught far more than his share of fish that day and while my reluctance to go all out might've kept me a little bit cleaner, in the end it was Kevin who ended up with the bragging rights.

Flipping through the old family albums, I came across a number of other pictures that could've easily been selected to grace the front cover. There were actually four other photos taken of us that day on the lake. Three of them depict Kevin, fish in tow, making a beeline toward the pickle bucket to stash away his prize. The fourth is a priceless shot of him wading knee-deep in water, reaching out to grab another one as it jumps quickly to avoid his grasp.

Another potential candidate shows us in the living room with my dad, proudly displaying a stringer full of pan fish. My father, wearing his worn out *Snap-On Tools* shirt and faded denim jeans, is situated carefully between us keeping the fish tails from dragging the floor. On the mantle behind us stands a figurine of a large oak tree that had been a gift from a family friend. Painted directly above the tree are the words "Country Bumpkins," a visual reminder of the day-care center my parents ran out of our home.

And finally, one of my personal favorites is a simple shot of Kevin hugging the stuffed bunny rabbit he'd just gotten that year for Easter. It was one of the first toys created that was able to play music (new technology back then), and this one played the tune "Here comes Peter Cottontail" whenever you squeezed his belly. I'm sure my mom thought it was just adorable and there's no doubt it was her idea to buy it for him. Kevin, around age four at the time, absolutely loved his new gift. He'd go around pressing its stomach over and over again, singing along with the tune until my parents finally made him stop.

One day he came inside with a puzzled look upon his face and handed the bunny over to my mother for inspection. It only took a minute for her to discover what was bothering him. It seems the mechanism that activated the music was permanently broken in the *on* position. No matter how hard she tried, she just couldn't seem to shut it off. Frustrated, she finally stuffed it inside my dad's top desk drawer to escape the sound and to see if he could fix it when he got home. Unfortunately for Kevin, my dad got to his desk before ever having a chance to talk with my mother. As soon as he entered the room, he began to search frantically for the source of that dreadful noise. My dad's ears had become so incredibly sensitive to what had now become the most annoying sound in the world, that he was able to locate that stuffed animal in no time.

Struggling furiously to shut it off he stormed outside, bunny in hand, to take care of this little problem once and for all. The look on Kevin's face was sheer terror as my father threw the toy upon his work table and reached quickly inside his toolbox. When his hand reappeared it had wrapped itself tightly around the handle of a three-pound sledge hammer. There was no doubt in anybody's mind what would come next. Scared half to death Kevin cried out, "Daddy, don't hurt my bunny!" but to no avail as the full force of that hammer came crashing down upon the table. All of a sudden, the noise was gone. Nobody spoke a word. After witnessing this disturbing event both Kevin and I were too afraid to utter a sound. But at least it was over. My dad stood victorious, the bunny had finally been defeated.

In this case a picture is not worth a thousand words. There is no way anyone could have imagined what happened just by looking at that photograph. Now that it's over, this incident has become one of my favorite memories, and even Kevin can laugh about what a psycho my dad was to destroy his stuffed bunny in such reckless fashion. However, after careful consideration I decided that this particular picture did not convey enough of the story behind it to make the final cut.

As you can see, narrowing down the field of possibilities to just one that would be used for the cover was not an easy process. There were a great number of photos that could've served as excellent examples of our southern heritage. In the end though, the picture affectionately referred to as "Our Redneck Fishing Trip" just couldn't be denied. It was such a perfect illustration of how we always seemed to stand out from the crowd, even in a small town like Lake City. Besides, it was taken in black & white by an actual employee of the *Lake City Reporter*. What more could I have possibly asked for in a cover photo?

In retrospect, I have come to realize just how interesting my life has been. Even today just thinking about some of those wild stories makes me laugh out loud. Some have been sad, some a little weird, but most of them are downright hilarious. Keep in mind that what you are reading actually happened. I assure you that everything you find in the pages ahead is one hundred percent true. Not even the names have been changed to protect the accused. And now, I am offering you the chance to relive those very experiences along with me as I take you on a personally guided tour of my life, *The Redneck Chronicles*.

1

"The West Virginia in Ya"

Before going much further, I should probably give you enough information about my parent's background as to set a proper foundation for the rest of the book. A brief overview of their life experiences will give you a better perspective on what it is that makes me tick. After all, a child's parents always leave a lasting impression on them, often carried beyond their adolescence and into adulthood. I am no different. The mark my mother and father branded upon me so many years ago has penetrated my subconscious mind forever. No matter how hard I may have tried to fight it before, I now realize the futility of attempting to deny your roots.

I have reached the conclusion that I am at least 50% redneck by birth. Having received half my DNA from my father assures me of that. He is a 100%, no doubt about it, bona fide backwoods hick. If you were to ever meet him on the street, you would have no trouble at all believing he fits the profile. The evidence against him is overwhelming.

He doesn't care much about his physical appearance or the clothes he wears, nor does he concern himself much with what other people think about it. His outfits often consist of hand me down t-shirts and old mesh baseball caps. Growing up, I remember his shirt pockets filled to maximum capacity with everything from cheap cigars to pens and notepads. Socks were no good unless they had two colored stripes and could be worn up over the calves during the summer.

Raised without much money, he became quite a packrat determined to save everything of value he could get his hands on. Now you must realize that in this context the word *value* may have a slightly different meaning than you're probably used to. In this instance, the most literal definition is as follows:

value—anything with potentially salvageable parts (commonly referred to as 'junk') that might be usable at some later date. Items must also be kept completely assembled so as to take up the most storage space possible. (i.e. nonworking lawnmowers, broken lamps, old bicycles, buckets of odd sized screws, etc.)

Never mind the fact that he could easily pick up any of those spare parts from the local hardware store dirt cheap. There's enough old junk crammed into his cluttered apartment that he could have his own multi-family garage sale every Saturday for three months straight. He's accumulated so much junk, that he actually rented a storage shed for $125 a month just to be able to keep it "safe". It finally dawned on him that the storage unit was costing him way too much money and he reluctantly decided to get rid of it. You should have seen his face that day when he had to dispose of all that stuff. It looked as if he'd just lost his best friend.

His affection for keeping old junk isn't the only thing that reveals his redneck nature. For example, even though he's now driving a late model Honda, he still keeps the beat up old multi-color Chevy pickup around for good measure. The body is bright red, but the truck was in an accident and the hood doesn't close properly. Unable to find the right color to match, he settled on a green one that he was able to pickup at a bargain. Unfortunately this still didn't solve the problem, so the bright red truck now has two yellow straps keeping the lime green hood from flying off into traffic. It's quite a sight. He fits nearly every stereotype in the book and yet appears completely oblivious to his plight. I suppose in his case ignorance really is bliss. If only I could be so lucky.

Born in the mountains of West Virginia, my father's heritage stretches back many generations. While visiting on a family vacation once, I remember my dad pointing out a small dirt road in the middle of nowhere bearing the family name. He was so proud. I can't say the same for myself though, as that beat up old street sign serves as a constant reminder of my undeniable southern lineage. A beacon of hope, so to speak, showing the way back home should I ever become lost on my journey through life.

Extended family is common in that part of the country and my father was no exception. His mother was very young when he was born and decided he'd be better off being raised by her aunt and uncle. Technically, this would have been his great aunt and great uncle, but whenever he refers to them its always 'grandma' and 'grandpa'. Part of the reason may be because they also took his mother in as their own when she was a small child. She occasionally made time to come and visit while he was growing up, but my dad never really had a close relationship with her until much later. Like any child, he'd always longed for the love and attention of his biological parents. It didn't help matters that his father was out of the picture before he was old enough to remember. There were a couple occasions when he tried to meet his dad but to no avail.

All of this eventually took its toll and although he loved his adopting parents deeply, the time would come for his departure. At the tender young age of only seventeen my dad enlisted in the United States Marine Corps. The conflict in Vietnam had become increasingly volatile, so with a strong sense of patriotism and perhaps a bit of youthful naivety, he volunteered to help defend democracy on foreign soil.

Marine Corps boot camp on Parris Island was extremely brutal back in those days. These brave young men were being prepared for war and the intensity of the training reflected the seriousness of the time. Dad was absolutely determined to make it through, and though he suffered tremendous physical and mental anguish in his brief time there, it paled in comparison to the horrors he would see in the months ahead.

While serving a tour of duty in Vietnam, my dad discovered that he and his father were both "in country" at the same time. They made contact and even planned to finally meet in person. But his father soon realized that due to certain military regulations one of them could leave the country immediately. And true to character, that's exactly what he did.

Somehow my parents managed to maintain a relationship while dad was overseas. When he returned to the states a position was available to become a drill instructor back at Parris Island. So after the proper training he and my mother moved to South Carolina, taking on the unenviable task of preparing new recruits to head overseas. There's no doubt the experiences of war changed my father in ways I can't possibly imagine. Nor is there any question of the lasting impact left upon him when faced with the challenge of preparing those brave young men for the atrocities of war.

There was never any doubt about dad's history. My mom though, now that was the real shocker. Any chance I had of being normal was gone the moment I discovered the truth about my mother. Come to find out, it was all some kind of giant cover up, apparently designed to delude my brother and I into believing she comes from a normal background. Nothing could be further from the truth. My own mother played us both for fools. I always figured it was still possible that the redneck side of me would end with my generation. I thought my children might still have an outside chance of being born normal. Maybe it was like in Biology class when we learned about Gregor Mendel, the father of modern genetics. If the redneck genes that dad passed on to me were recessive, and the other genes were dominant, then maybe we still had a shot. But mom blew that theory to shreds when she revealed her true identity.

There is nothing obvious about my mother that would give away her redneck nature. That's probably why it was so easy for her to keep Kevin and me in the dark for so many years. She is very well groomed, taking care to bathe herself at least once a day. All of her teeth are still in tact and not only does she brush them regularly, she even makes a point to visit the dentist on a yearly basis. She's never smoked cigarettes, or cigars for that matter, and I can only remember her having a drink once or twice in my lifetime. Can you believe it? I have a redneck for a mom and I've never even seen her drunk. On the surface, there isn't much about her that might indicate she too had been given the redneck gene. We may never have learned the truth if it weren't for an unlikely slip of the tongue.

It wasn't until after a recent trip to New York with her sisters that we finally began to uncover the truth. Her family had much history there and when she went back to visit she began digging into the past. The three of them were sitting around the kitchen table, chatting about their adventure when it all came out. It seems that while investigating her family history, she came to discover that somewhere way back in the lineage was a couple that entered into wedlock despite being previously related as first cousins. What a shock it was for me to discover that it was actually her side of the family tree, not my dad's, where the branches didn't fork. Maybe we could prune it back somehow, let a new branch grow out instead. Fortunately, we are not direct descendants of the individuals in question. Thank goodness. At least I don't have to worry about my kids being born with seven toes or a third nipple.

Other than the marriage of her already related ancestors, a widely known redneck stereotype, a deeper look at her childhood offered even more clues to her hidden identity. Born in rural upstate New York, she moved with the rest of the family to Florida while she was still rather young. And what a family is was. She was the fourth of five children with two older brothers and both an older and younger sister. The boys were very close in age and fought a lot with each other. According to my mom, her father spent most of his time at home drinking beer and watching television. This led to an environment that was often verbally and sometimes physically abusive. She can recall many instances when one of the boys would backtalk their dad and he would punch them repeatedly telling them how worthless they were. As for her mother, she did the best she could but was frequently out on the town, trying her best to escape the situation if only for a little while. The harsh reality was that there were five children in that house who would carry the wounds of abuse and neglect for many years to come.

I remember how violently ill her father was when came to visit us in Georgia. He couldn't even stand on his own two feet, much less walk around on his own accord. I'll never forgot how frail and weak he seemed as my parents made me help him go to the bathroom. I actually had to hold my grandfather up so he could urinate in the toilet without falling down. This was the first time I'd seen him in many years and I thought his weakness might be a result of getting old. The other possibility I entertained was that he was sick from all the drinking. It turns out that the real reason for his physical condition was actually due to a lack of alcohol. I found out later that the family brought him up from Florida and placed him in a detoxification program at the hospital. His alcoholism had reached such a dangerous level that if they didn't do something, he wouldn't have survived much longer.

Despite the challenges she faced in her youth my mother grew into an exceptional woman. She provided me with a solid foundation, offering unconditional love and support. Her two sisters did a great job with their lives as well, especially when you consider the circumstances they faced growing up. That's the thing about being a redneck. People don't usually expect you to accomplish much. The apple doesn't fall too far from the tree you know. I'm just glad mom didn't buy into any of that garbage. She always set the standards high for us boys, expecting us to succeed in anything we set our hearts upon. Sadly, her brothers weren't so lucky. They internalized a great deal of pain and were ultimately unable to handle the struggles life threw their way.

Chris was the second of two boys born into my mother's family. There's no doubt he harbored tremendous anger for the years of abuse, even after their father had passed away. Upon his passing, the house remained vacant for a while as the family grieved and worked to resolve this unpleasant situation. They realized major repair would be needed if they expected to get a fair price. After putting the place back together, they returned home to Atlanta and promptly listed the property for sale with a Florida real estate agent. Rather than trying to keep it, they felt it would be best to sell the home splitting the money evenly amongst the siblings. That's when the agent called my aunt informing her that Chris had moved his stuff into the house. He was apparently throwing wild parties with absolutely no concern about the condition of the newly refurbished residence. Come to find out, he even sent away credit card applications that had been mailed to his deceased father's address. Since he'd been given the same birth name, he was able to run up thousands of dollars of debt to finance his drug and alcohol addiction. It was quite a mess to untangle.

Chris was very unstable and a bit of a loose cannon. There was one time he actually pulled a pistol on my father. Thankfully, dad was experienced with life threatening situations and was able to talk him into putting the gun down before anyone got hurt. Of course he was intoxicated at the time and probably hopped up on pills of some sort. But that didn't make him any less dangerous and I'm just glad my dad was there to help. Maybe his sons will have better luck breaking the chain.

Elbert was the first born son and as a result bore the brunt of his father's abuse. In spite of this, he grew into a fine young man and fared alright for a while. Like my dad, he enlisted in the military when he heard that war had broken out in Vietnam. He chose the Army and became a crew chief aboard a U.S. helicopter. Part of the reason for his decision was undoubtedly an attempt to escape the ghosts of his past. Going to war may seem like a strange place to run, but he was also a patriot at heart and felt it was the right thing to do. Little did he know it then, but the things he'd witness overseas would make his childhood seem like a walk in the park.

It took some time and enormous effort, but he was finally coming to grips with his past. He met a wonderful woman with two terrific boys who he fell in love with immediately. It looked like things were turning around as they exchanged vows and started a new life together. Everything was fine for the first three years until the United States entered into military conflict again, this time in the Middle East. Elbert's wife called our house in tears to let us know of his death. It seems he had been drinking heavily one night and accidentally overdosed on painkillers. My father believes it was intentional, the constant reminder of war proving too much to take. But we'll never know the real circumstances surrounding his untimely passing. What we do know is how great a tragedy it was since he seemed to have finally found a sense of peace in those young boys. He wanted the two them to have the life he never had. I guess in the end it wasn't enough to save him. Or was it?

Needless to say, my mother faced her share of difficulties in life. But isn't that the way it is with all redneck families? Maybe families of all kinds have their share of skeletons hidden in the closet. The relatives nobody talks about or even considers part of the family. Some people even seem to be embarrassed by their own family. That's what makes rednecks so unique. We take care of our own. And I know that despite their colorful history together, if Chris were to call any of his sisters needing help they would do whatever they could to help out. That's how they've always been, and it won't stop with her generation. Like it or not we are a family, and I am my brother's keeper.

At least now I can understand what my mom saw in my dad. For a while there I thought he hurried and married her before she was old enough to know any better. After all, she was only sixteen when they got hitched and she believed he was the man of her dreams. And he was, at least for a while. Besides, she was extremely anxious to leave home and start a fresh new life all her own. How's the old expression go, "Out of the frying pan, into the skillet?"

Now I know what you're probably thinking. Just how fortunate can one guy be? What did I ever do to have fate smile upon me so kindly? Truth be told, I didn't always have the same kind of unbridled enthusiasm for being a redneck that I do today. In fact, there was actually a time when I resented my family background. Kevin and I even came up with a catchy phrase to describe our inborn tendency toward certain unwanted behavioral traits. Whenever we see each other displaying one of these unique characteristics, we are always quick to jump in and say "It's the West Virginia in ya". To get the full affect, it must be said with a bit of a southern twang, the last three words run together as one. We stumbled onto it one day while joking around about our past and it just kind of stuck. It wasn't until much later that it gained enough notoriety to be included here. A word of advice for anyone who might be considering adopting this catchy phrase into their own vernacular, it's only meant to poke fun at specific redneck behaviors. These words carry great weight and should be used with extreme caution. Spoken the wrong way, to the wrong person, or with a heavy northern accent could cause serious repercussions for which I cannot be held accountable.

Born into such a unique family has had a profound effect on the outcome of my life. For example, most folks have never been lucky enough to experience the great taste of true southern cuisine. How many people can honestly say they've eaten fried squirrel. A bit greasy at first, this "tree rodent" is actually considered quite a delicacy in some circles. Other favorite dishes include, fried bananas, chicken hearts, chicken gizzards, fried tomatoes, fried liver (beef), pickled pigs feet, turtle soup (usually snapper), fried zucchini, etc. Of all the things my parents ate, I had the hardest time understanding the cow liver, despite the fact that I still have no idea where the gizzard comes from. But the liver, it had no taste, just this strange pasty texture that made it even harder to get down. Oh, and the other thing mom would eat that I never understood was turkey necks. She still eats them today. My question is, what in the world do you eat? I mean, it's a neck for goodness sake. Not exactly the meatiest part of the turkey. In fact, I'm still not sure if there is any meat on that particular region of the bird. She swears there is, but she always buys them in bulk often eating many at a time.

Often, the food we ate came right out of mom's garden or from recent fishing and hunting trips. Growing up poor, dad was never one to waste and if he could get food on the table for the cost of bait or ammo that was fine with him. No doubt with his superior outdoorsman skills we'd never go hungry. This reminds me of my very favorite story of his from my youth. Believe me, there were many and he told them so often I could repeat most of them line for line. But for integrity's sake, this story will be quoted directly from his mouth to these pages so nothing is lost in translation.

"I decided to take Brent squirrel hunting one day. You know, start teaching him about gun safety and how to get around in the woods and track the animals. We had permission to go back in behind this old farmer's field back in the tree lines and stuff. We went back in there and I showed Brent some marks on the trees where some turkeys had scratched and some rabbit "stuff" was on the ground where they'd been to the bathroom. We were looking for squirrels but the only ones we could see were too far off to shoot. The trip was winding down because as the sun gets higher the squirrels tend to be less active. So we had stepped out into the edge of this cornfield that had been mowed down. They had taken the corn and made it into fodder for cows, of course when they do that there's corn and stuff still left on the ground. Well, we got out to the edge and all of a sudden about eight or ten turkeys were caught thirty or forty yards out in the field and they started running toward the tree line. They took off up into the air and when they did they were still only about thirty yards away from us and they were flying right straight across our path. So I cocked back the .410, pulled it up and aimed it out straight in front of this turkey, the biggest one in the bunch, squeezing off a round that hit him. When it did he just crapped all over everything and kept right on flying, it didn't even slow him down. That made me mad as hell so when we got out of the woods I went on to the house and went straight out and bought me a twelve-gauge shotgun 'cause I wasn't ever going to let that happen to me again."

People always break into hysterical laughter every time he shares this wild experience of ours with family and friends. I've often wondered what they found to be more amusing, the story itself or my dad's lively reenactment. Either way, it has become one of my fondest memories to date and the funny thing about it is that I don't even remember being there.

The pairing of my mother and father together and allowing them to create offspring makes me believe God really does have a sense of humor. Looking back, it's easy to see how combining such a diverse group of personalities together under one roof would inevitably lead to trouble. But before we could get started on our creative journey through life, my parents needed a place they could call home. They weren't just looking for any old spot to live. No, these newlyweds needed a place where they could settle down and start a family. Of all the places in the world they could have raised us, I can think of no better backdrop than the small little town in Florida that forever changed my life.

2

"Small Town Living"

Shortly after tying the knot, my folks were looking for a good place to settle down and raise their new family. They'd only been married a few years when my mother got pregnant with me. Before I entered the picture, they moved all over Florida's east coast taking on whatever adventure life threw their way. But now, with the added responsibility of a small child to care for, they were intent on finding a place to call home. The challenge of getting stable work weighed heavily into their decision, and we traveled all over the state searching for the perfect location.

Dad was having trouble keeping a job due to an inability to hold his tongue. Needless to say, there were more than a few occasions when he separated from his employer shouting colorful metaphors while giving them the finger. In his words, he has absolutely no tolerance for 'butt-holes' and he doesn't 'take no crap from no one'. With such a young family though, this might not have been the best strategy as he bounced around from job to job. Things finally seemed to be turning around when a small credit outfit caught his interest.

That's what prompted the move to Lake City. Dad's position with the new company was located there and since mom had no real ties to her job it was an easy decision to make. Living in such a small town would be an adjustment, but my mother was weary from moving so much and looking very forward to settling down. They were also quite excited about dad's new career, especially with the opportunity for advancement it offered. He'd never had a job he liked this much before and things seemed to be headed the right direction.

As for mom, she was busy getting used to her new environment. And what an environment it turned out to be. Like any small town, there wasn't a whole lot available in the way of entertainment. For the younger crowd, the local skating rink was a popular hangout. Dad would take me there occasionally and was always anxious to show off his roller skating prowess. Some of the older town folk spent much of their time in the local bar, cleverly named *The Dew Drop Inn.*

Sometimes dad would take me there with him too. I guess it's never too early to start learning the fundamentals of playing pool. At least that's what he always told my mother. As for the daylight hours, fishing and hunting were among the top priorities.

There were plenty of freshwater lakes in town and dad loved to go fishing in them. He even went so far as buying a little aluminum boat so we could get to all the honey holes. If you're not familiar with fishing lingo, the term "honey hole" refers to a fishing hotspot where you either catch a lot of fish or you catch something that's worth mounting. Funny thing about that is the only fish he ever took to the taxidermist was a largemouth bass he caught just a couple feet off shore.

We fished for everything, pan fish, bass, catfish, and pretty much anything else that would take the bait. Nothing ever went to waste. Whatever we caught that day at the lake would most likely be served that night for dinner, accompanied by a side of coleslaw and homemade french-fries. Pan fish, like blue-gill and bream, were the most common and were also the easiest to catch. Just throw a cricket or worm on your hook, toss it into the water and wait. As soon as the bobber disappears you jerk back hard on the rod setting the hook. If successful, you are then ready to reel in your prize. And the fish weren't the only ones to take the bait.

Kevin reminded me about how my dad taught him a "secret" technique for catching bullfrogs. First, you hook the cricket right beneath its collar. This way it's still able to jump around freely, tempting the frogs into action. Next you grab a small piece of fishing line and use it to dangle the cricket on the ground underneath the dock. If you were patient enough, one of these enormous frogs would eventually lash out their tongue swallowing the cricket hook and all. I realize you may very well be thinking, "Why would anyone want to catch a bullfrog?" Granted it's not a question without merit. The answer of course is that giant bullfrogs have giant frog legs, considered a delicacy in many parts of the south. But not in our kitchen as mom refused to cook them on her stove. Kevin was terribly disappointed by the news as he'd returned home with an entire bucket full of frogs. But everyone has their limits and this was hers, end of story. To our dismay, this would be both the first and the last time we ever fished for bullfrogs.

On another fishing excursion, I was around six or seven years old at the time, my dad tried his best to get me eaten by a twelve foot alligator. Let me explain. We were out fishing from his boat on Water Town Lake one day, when he noticed a baby alligator swimming alongside us in the water. The aluminum john boat was small, barely sticking out of the water, so dad grabbed his net and scooped the creature up to get a better look. At first my dad was thrilled to get an up close look at the little guy. But I'll never forget the look of sheer terror on his face as he heard it start squealing for help. Just then, a huge tail splashed down in the water just a few yards away. Alligators are not very aggressive creatures by nature. There were many occasions when we'd shoo them off the dock in the morning so we could go fishing. Never did they show even a hint of aggression toward us or anyone else that came near them. But this time was different. We were messing with its young and there was no telling what would happen next. Dad moved faster than you can imagine as he dumped that baby gator back in the lake. Luckily, he managed to get the motor running quickly, speeding us away before the boat was capsized and I was turned into gator bait. Needless to say, we didn't go fishing on that lake again for quite a while.

Besides the adventures we had in the great outdoors, there were lots of other activities to keep us busy. One of the best things about living in Florida is that there was hardly any winter at all. By the time fall ended it seemed like spring had already begun. The flip side to that was seeing snow only once in fifteen years, but those winter sports are all so overrated anyway. Seems to me people are just making due with what they've got. If there's snow on the ground for months at a time, you have to find something worthwhile to use it for. Either that or stay cooped up indoors three months out of the year. But having a long summer, now that's the way to go.

Naturally with the benefit of such beautiful weather we spent a great deal of time around water. The beach was only an hour away and mom loved to take weekend getaways every chance she got. Surprisingly, there was really only one public spot to go swimming in town. I'm sure there must have been at least a couple neighborhood pools around somewhere, but not on my street. As a result, many weekend days were spent lounging around the pool at the local KOA Kampground. It wasn't much, but for just a few bucks mom could take Kevin and me swimming for hours. Plus, keeping us occupied gave her the opportunity to lay out on the lawn chairs while working on her tan. It was a win-win situation for all of us.

You know I don't ever remember dad getting in the pool with us. Sure he'd wade out into the ocean when we visited the beach, but not without his trusty fishing pole in hand. I guess he just wasn't much of a swimmer. Kind of a shame too since he could've easily used his belly as a flotation device. There wasn't much fat anywhere else on his body, it all just migrated to his midsection. He had no butt either. I don't mean to suggest that it was simply smaller than average. His rear end was completely nonexistent. Seriously, when viewed from the side it looked like his back extended straight down to his calves. Mom used to say it looked like someone smacked him real hard on the bottom pushing his butt out into his belly, always good for a laugh from us boys. Dad was pretty good natured about it all, blaming the size of his gut on mom's great cooking.

One summer there was rumor of plans to build a water park right off the interstate exit. News spread quickly and an air of excitement began to fill the area. It's all the kids at school were talking about. Massive water slides, Olympic size swimming pools, everyone was looking forward to the possibilities. As it turned out they completed the project that winter and the water park was open in time for summer. We were about to explode with anticipation as mom turned into the parking lot for the very first time. As she looked for a spot to park we could already see the top of the slide and couldn't wait to get inside. *Fun Unlimited*, what an incredibly appropriate name. Not only did this entertainment venue boast a giant water slide, but it was also home to a gift shop, video arcade, and a real live alligator farm.

The gift shop was rather small specializing in all sorts of trinkets reminiscent of the park. Choosing a location so close to the freeway allowed them to attract visitors from neighboring counties. Providing them with items from the gift shop was a great way to remember their experience, not to mention a terrific opportunity to increase the owner's bottom line. Novelty items like alligator key chains flew off the shelves as everyone seemed impressed with the offerings.

After paying admission and passing through the gift shop the water slide immediately came into view. It required the use of a padded mat to navigate your way down. One side of the mat was extremely slick while the other was callous and rough. Which side you laid against the floor of the slide determined how fast you traveled down the ride. After much experimentation, my friends and I figured out that if you wrapped the mat tightly around your body, keeping both your legs and head up off the floor, you could sometimes move fast enough to cause a collision midway down the slide. It became kind of a challenge amongst my peers, each of us trying our hardest to crash recklessly into the person going before us. My personal best was slamming into my buddy as he rounded the first turn. However I must confess that I'd never have caught him so quickly if not for taking off early, before the lifeguard instructed.

Besides the swimming pool, up on the hill was the coolest arcade I'd ever seen. They had four pinball machines, Donkey Kong, Ms. Pac Man, and many other hot games. In the corner of the room was a jukebox that cranked so loud you could hear it all the way down by the pool. In fact, I was thirteen years old hanging out in the water when I first heard *Panama* by Van Halen blaring from the loud speakers of the arcade.

As I mentioned before, *Fun Unlimited* was not your ordinary run of the mill amusement center. Actually, it was really more like two parks combined into one. Of course there were the popular attractions like the swimming pool and water slide. But there was also a section of the park devoted entirely to displaying wild life. In the right hand corner of the parking lot stood an enormous alligator head. The mouth of this great creature sat wide open, inviting visitors to walk through the rows of lifelike teeth and into the rest of the park.

Upon entering the facility, the first thing you noticed was the many alligators spread throughout the area. The second thing that came to mind was the incredible lack of protection in place to keep them from eating you alive. This was a bit unnerving at first. Call me crazy, but a two-foot high wooden fence consisting of a couple plywood slats and a wooden stake every six or eight feet was not what I considered "tourist friendly". Come to find out though the alligators were extremely docile and well trained and would never hurt one of the park visitors. Oddly this did little to put my mind at ease and I always exercised great caution around the reptiles preferring to steer clear of that section of the park altogether. I could just see the local headlines "Young boy swallowed whole by escaped alligator." Not the kind of publicity that would be good for business. Then again, people are strange. Who knows what kind of notoriety the place would receive for an event of this magnitude. The press would have been in a total frenzy. Thankfully, nothing like this ever happened before they redesigned the alligator's cages.

It never ceased to amaze me how fascinated some people were over a single captive animal. I'm not kidding. They would wait for hours for this little otter to climb to the top of his concrete home. Once he reached the summit they would throw food, yell encouragement, and do anything else they could to coax him to slide down the ramp back into the water. To be fair, it was kind of neat to watch…the first time. After that it was the same old thing time and time again. And it's not like he complied often with their requests. Often, he'd sit there openly defiant, toying with the emotions of those poor little rednecks. Sometimes I'd stand nearby, getting as much of a kick out of watching them as they did by watching the otter.

Overall, the arrival of *Fun Unlimited* was a huge hit. I think we went back to KOA a few times after that but only when mom was tight on money. It was the perfect place to spend a lazy summer day out lounging by the pool. The new park also provided a much needed boost to the local economy. But what about those few months of the year when the weather wasn't good enough for poolside activities?

Every year near the beginning of fall, signs began popping up all over town announcing the upcoming dates of the county fair. This always generated a great deal of excitement in my family. It was my favorite time of year. Maybe it was the fact that the fair only came around once each year that got my adrenaline flowing. Whatever it was, my parents were never happy to see those flyers go up because they knew it marked the beginning of my campaign. I would pour every ounce of energy I could muster into lobbying them to go the first night. And it didn't stop there. They knew that after the first trip was over I'd immediately be bugging them to go back again the next night. Most of the time I'd hit them up right in the parking lot. After the first couple years they became quite good at these annual negotiations and usually got out of it with only two or three visits.

Part of the appeal of the county fair was the incredible setup of rides. The Ferris wheel was our favorite for a while. That is until I grew tall enough to ride the other exciting attractions. Bumper cars, tilt-a-whirl, and other rides Kevin was still too short too ride became my personal playground. It was my first real taste of freedom as mom let me run around with my friends while she and dad entertained my brother. That's when I discovered the ride to end all rides, *The Gravitron*. Shaped like a giant flying saucer, it looked like something straight out of a science fiction movie with neon lights so bright you could spot them from anywhere on the fairgrounds. It was brand new and so popular that the line to ride seemed to go on forever. I didn't care. I was going to get my turn if I had to wait all night.

And wait we did. It took us over an hour to reach the front of the line. But now our patience had finally paid off. We carefully navigated the metal steps as we stepped aboard. Inside was one big circular walkway that wound itself around a DJ stand situated in the middle of the room. The outer wall was slightly angled with a number of individual pads firmly attached every few feet. Everyone scrambled to find a spot next to their friends as the DJ instructed us to locate and lean our backs against one of the pads on the wall. Strapping ourselves in, he did a quick walk through to ensure everyone was securely in place. Then he returned to his booth, cranked the 80's music up real loud, and told everyone to get ready. It started to spin slowly at first and the multi-colored lights were now flashing around the dark black room. As the speed increased the pads began to slide up the wall, taking us with them, due to the G-force being created by the spinning. It was like being suspended in midair. My friend Poco was busy trying to raise his arm off the wall, only to have it come slamming down hard beside him. We were having the time of our lives, but after just a few short minutes it was over.

Getting off the ride I noticed my body felt a bit strange. It was nothing I could put my finger on, just an overall uneasy feeling likely caused by the level of pressure on the ride. I was trying my best to shake it off while Poco was going on about how awesome *The Gravitron* had been. He was full of enthusiasm and because he didn't want to wait to ride again, persuaded me to jump on the *Tilt-A-Whirl* instead. This was a big mistake.

Over the course of my lifetime I have been sick many times. But nothing would compare to how I felt that night at the fair. This used to be one of my all time favorite rides. After that night it got bumped to the bottom of the list. The *Tilt-A-Whirl* was yet another ride that involved a heavy dose of spinning. The cart itself spun around and was attached to a track with other carts that rotated in a bigger circle. If that weren't enough, the track was also tilted (as the name implies) making it easier for the passengers to spin themselves faster. I think my friends were trying to get into the *Guinness Book of World Records* for the fastest spinning *Tilt-A-Whirl* cart in the world. They might've been close but oddly enough there were no judges anywhere to witness this amazing feat. It took me nearly three hours to recuperate to the point of being able to walk. Needless to say I now have a healthy respect for all rides that harness the power of gravity.

For all the fun we had on the rides at the fair, the experience wasn't complete without trying your luck at the many games available. Some of them were incredibly easy, like trying to toss a ping pong ball into a goldfish bowl with colored water. Mom loved that game and I can't ever remember leaving the fair without a goldfish of our very own. Others games were not so simple and due to their higher lever of difficulty, the more challenging ones lured participants in with the promise of gigantic prizes for the winners. They could get away with offering more expensive rewards because people rarely won. Their system worked much like the principle that continues to rake in millions of dollars for the state lottery every year. If the prize is big enough, it doesn't matter how likely you are to win. People will play anyway. And occasionally, just like in the lottery, somebody would win. When that happened it only added fuel to the fire, because now there was living proof that it could be done. Seeing news of someone hitting a $100 million jackpot gets people excited. Likewise, carrying around a giant stuffed teddy bear at the county fair attracts a lot of attention too.

My dad was the king of beating these games and every year mom would always have her arms around a huge stuffed animal by night's end. You can't imagine how many people would come up to us asking him where he won such a fabulous prize. It was the same answer every time. "I won it at the *Milk Toss* game." He was always quick to point out that unlike the other games of chance this one was more a matter of skill. People never seemed to get tired of hearing him describe his wining technique. "The first thing you need to realize is that the softball is barely big enough to fit through the milk can. That means if it reaches the hole at too sharp an angle it will bounce out and you will lose. You have to loft the ball perfectly over the can so that it drops almost straight down through the hole. That's the only way to beat that game. It can be done, but it's not easy. Since three tosses costs five bucks, my suggestion is that you go back home and practice first before playing for real."

With his guidance I was able to become quite a *Milk Toss* player in my own right. I guess you could say he passed the legacy on to me. It didn't come without a price. On many afternoons I could be found tossing softballs at one of dad's old milk cans. I was determined to succeed and it wasn't long before it was my face those carnies came to fear. They eventually wised up and began hanging the animals over the center of the booth, right above the milk cans. The prizes were so big and hung down so low, that it was impossible to get the necessary loft on the ball to win the game. What a racquet. Oh well, it was fun while it lasted and I'll never forget those days at the county fair.

Another annual event taking place in the fall was the Olustee Festival. This was a celebration of the Civil War battle of Olustee fought just outside town. I think the South may have actually lost the battle, but that didn't stop us from having a good time. The streets were cleared early in the day to make way for the parade. All I can remember was getting candy tossed to us from the floats and the Shriners riding around like maniacs in their miniature cars. The festival itself took place in the middle of the day with plenty of food and fun for the whole family. There were grilled hamburgers and fried turkey legs. Fresh cooked funnel cakes were also a crowd favorite. It was easy to see who'd eaten one by the white powdered sugar smeared all over their face.

Vendors lined the streets offering arts and crafts of all kinds. One guy who specialized in woodworking captured the young market when he started producing rubber band guns. The kids who had them ran around shooting the ones who didn't causing quite a line to form at his booth. He also figured out how popular *Snap-N-Pops* would be and was able to capitalize from the battle being waged in the streets. Kind of ironic don't you think?

The climax of the weekend was the reenactment of the Battle of Olustee. The whole town turned out to observe the spectacle. For a town without much money they sure pulled out all the stops. Authentic replicas of weaponry were provided to every participating "soldier". The uniforms appeared so realistic they could've been pulled right off the troop's own backs. But what really got the crowd's attention were the cannons. When shots were fired real smoke poured from inside as they made the loudest boom you've ever heard. After it was all said and done, amidst boos from the audience, the Union won the battle every time. I never did understand why so many people took offense to something that happened so long ago.

Despite the limited population we never seemed to be at a loss for quality entertainment. If there wasn't anything exciting going on my parents would always think of something. Don't get me wrong, there were plenty of things around to keep us occupied. But when you're a young boy, any free time on your hands can lead to trouble. And it was Lake City that proved to be the perfect backdrop for our mischievous ways. Growing up in small town provided me with a unique perspective on life. It was also the home to many of my most outrageous experiences. Most of which I will never forget.

3

"The Early Years"

When my mother brought Kevin home from the hospital the first time, I was in no mood to share my parents with a new baby. Why should he get all the attention? For over four years there was only me. As her firstborn child she made a habit of spoiling me rotten. That is until that little punk invaded my territory. His arrival into the family altered my whole world in an instant. This was no subtle change either. It was more like a throw everything you've ever known right out the window because it doesn't work that way anymore kind of change. Anytime there is already one child in a family, the only thing a new baby does is upset the natural balance. It had taken me all of my four years to get my parents trained when Kevin entered the picture, more than anxious to steal my thunder. Not only would I be expected to share my parents with this new kid, I was going to have to share my toys with him too. Enough is enough. Toys are where I draw the line. So, based entirely on petty jealously, I set out to make his life growing up a living hell. After having me for a big brother, he would be sorry he was ever born.

To be honest, I can't even remember a time when we didn't fight as kids. My mind is filled with so many wonderful memories of kicking Kevin's little butt. No form of abuse was out of bounds in my mind. Anything that didn't kill him was fair game. He was under the watchful eye of my mother the first few years of his life. Everyone seemed to shower him with attention. We had visitors I'd never met come by just to see Kevin. What about me, wasn't anyone going to notice me? It was as if I had suddenly become invisible. With so many people around it was impossible for me to exact my revenge. But I knew that with enough patience, my time would eventually come.

The effect of a new child in the house was barely wearing off when I started school. Going to the first grade was like being a tiny minnow thrown headfirst into a big fish pond. Most of the kids in the other grades had gone there the year before and knew the ropes. For me though, the first year in elementary school was intimidating. There were lots of bigger kids there, especially the fifth graders. And the school was also much larger than what I'd experienced in kindergarten. Not to mention the fact that I was much shorter than most of the other children in class. This is also the age where kids start to notice each other's differences. Certain things tend to stick out. Naturally, if you are dumb, smart, slow, ugly, redneck, poor, tall, short, fat, skinny, nerdy, or dorky there was a pretty good chance you were going to get picked on by the other kids.

As for me, I was short, skinny, with red hair, freckles, and big pointy ears. Of all this, the big ears bothered me the most. I can remember staring into the mirror pushing my ears back against my head. Mom would constantly reassure me that they weren't "that big", but I knew better. It's not like I was blind, I could see my own reflection. I would find out later of a surgical procedure that might've fixed my little problem. But even if they'd heard of it, there's no way my parents could've spent the money on something like that. Besides, mom was of the opinion that it didn't really matter what other people thought. She said I looked perfectly fine, but I thought she was full of malarkey. What do parents know anyway? It did matter what the other kids in school thought. At least it did to me.

On top of my physical imperfections, my parents soon began having financial struggles and I had to get free lunch at school. In those days there was a special card you gave the cafeteria ladies so that you wouldn't be charged for your food. The problem with that system was the card was bright orange and every other kid in line knew you were on the program. It's not like many of their parents were in much better financial shape than mine, but that didn't stop the teasing. And their comments cut me deep.

It's not like we had any control over it. Released from Credit Thrift, my dad was having a hard time finding a new job. Mom dealt with the responsibility of being the sole breadwinner in the house. It's not like dad wasn't trying to earn a living. He was doing all sorts of odd jobs to scrape extra money together but it was still tough. One of his ideas involved creating a twenty foot extension cord that enabled him to work on broken dryers in the backyard. He'd find them sitting out by the side of the road for the trash collector. Most times the only thing wrong with them was a burnt heating element. The part only cost a couple bucks to replace and he could sell the refurbished machines for fifty or seventy five dollars. Not a bad profit for an out of work ex-marine.

After a while I just got used to the ribbing dished out by my fellow classmates. Anyway, it didn't take long before I discovered they were just as vulnerable to hurtful criticism as me. I also learned that with my quick wit putdowns came rather naturally to me. What began as a necessary defense mechanism soon evolved into an emotional shield that served to protect my fragile ego. In time I learned that striking first blood was a great strategy to prevent incoming remarks. It wasn't until much later that I finally decided to turn over a new leaf.

It was in first grade that I met Poco, who would become one of my best friends. We got along right off the bat and hung out together as much as possible. If you're wondering where he got such a strange name, it was his mother's idea. He told me she heard it in a movie once and, much to his dismay, it stuck with her. In the film though, he said it was actually the name of a dog. I thought it was odd that he'd been named after a four legged animal, but felt it best not to press the matter any further. His real name was actually Roger, but thanks to his mother everyone had always called him Poco. Whenever he got a new teacher in school, he'd have to inform her of what he preferred to go by during the initial roll call. It always drew funny looks from the class and I'm sure he didn't enjoy having to repeat the same process again the next year.

Those days in elementary school were something else. I believe it was in the third grade that I first learned how to do a penny drop. This was a huge hit with the other kids and was always sure to draw a crowd. We just had to be careful not to let the teachers catch us. If they did, it would be off to the principal's office for sure. The technique involved was simple in theory but much harder in actual practice. Most of the kids were too scared to even attempt such a daredevil act. Not me. I was fearless and just beginning to hit my prime, making quite a habit out of hurting myself in the process.

It started well before I started school. Like the time I was only three years old on a family trip to the park. My mom was swinging in one of those heavy wooden swings they used to have on the playground. I walked right behind the swing as it came crashing down into my face knocking me clean off my feet. She passed out cold from shock as the blood gushed out of my forehead near my left eye. Dad covered the wound with his shirt to stop the bleeding, rushing me immediately to the hospital. That was my first trip to the emergency room, but it wouldn't be my last. Considering how often I was involved in risky activities, it's amazing they didn't give me my own room.

Because of my mom's daycare center, our backyard was home to a variety of outdoor playground equipment providing the perfect training ground for me to hone my skills. The daycare had long been shut down, but the equipment still remained. Climbing trees became second nature and walking across the top of the monkey bars was a breeze. For a while, I'd only cross barefoot to maximize the sensitivity also giving me the best chance to avoid injury. It didn't take long though before I was practically running back and forth, even with both my shoes on. There was no doubt I was in desperate need of a new challenge. That's when I spotted the old swing-set sitting in the corner of our yard. It was perfect. There was only one bar stretching across the top, meaning it would take every ounce of balance in my body if I was to succeed. It was also a bit higher than my other stunts, requiring an increased level of concentration to go along with a steady foot. Looking down could spell immediate disaster, but I was ready and able. Conquering that decaying lawn ornament became my reason for living and I set out bravely on my new mission.

Finding a way up was the first challenge. I could just climb right up one of the side legs, but that looked difficult and I might get hurt before even reaching the top. Luckily, the swing-set was situated only a few short feet away from one of the big pecan trees in the yard. One of its limbs stretched right over my intended target. It looked to be close enough to reach so off I charged. Getting to the edge of the limb was child's play. Navigating my way onto the bar was only slightly harder as I stood upright still hanging onto the tree with both hands.

My feet didn't quite fit on the bar and I ended up turning them around sideways to get a better grip. It sure seemed a lot higher from that perspective than it did with both feet planted on solid ground. There was a brief moment of weakness when I almost chickened out. Regaining my composure, I focused intently on the bar beneath my feet and gently let go of the branch. One foot after the other, slow and steady I began moving toward my goal. I wasn't really scared of heights per se, but the fear of falling certainly bothered me. Only a few more steps remained when my foot landed in a wet spot, causing me to instantly lose my balance. It seems the morning dew got the better of me that day as I came crashing to the ground. But not before hitting my leg on the jagged metal edge protruding out from one of the rides. Again dad came running out to assist me in my time of crisis. Mom would have done it but there's something about the sight of her son's blood everywhere that makes her irrational.

The next time I had the privilege of seeing the inside of those hospital walls was with a short piece of wood nailed to my hand. We were playing baseball in the backyard when an errant throw pulled me off the base. Diving for the ball I fell headfirst into a pile of wood dad had stacked out beside the shed. Not all of the nails had been pulled from the boards yet and my hand found a rusty one that happened to be pointed in my direction. It went straight through the flesh as I found myself nailed securely to a piece of lumber about two feet long. Naturally I screamed bloody murder as my father ran outside to see what was wrong. Seeing my punctured hand, he wrapped a towel around it and tossed me in the truck again. He didn't even bother removing the board first as we raced down the turning lane at sixty miles an hour. You'd think they'd put us on some kind of frequent customer plan or something as often as I was coming in. Some of the nurses even got to know me on a first name basis.

It's strange, but the first time I got into a fist fight at school was the one time I didn't get hurt. At least not in the physical sense, my wounded ego took quite a beating that day. It happened right after the last bell rang, alerting the student body it was time to go home. I was heading down the covered walkway to meet my dad who was picking me up from school that day, when another kid came up and started bothering me. The first thing he asked was what grade I was in. When I replied he said he couldn't believe anybody as short as me could possibly be in the fifth grade. As it turns out, he was only in the fourth grade but stood a full head taller than me. He was also a heavyset kid and must've outweighed me by at least forty pounds. That's not saying much considering I had yet to hit my growth spurt. Come to think of it, I'm 29 years old and still waiting for those few extra inches of height. I'm beginning to think it might never happen. At any rate, let's get back to the story.

Now I was never one for physical altercations and tried to avoid fighting whenever possible. What I did with Kevin was more like roughhousing, since we never threw any punches and certainly never intended to hurt each other. Not bad anyway. But this was different. That bully kept pushing me around and just wouldn't leave me alone. My dad, who'd been waiting in the parking lot, came looking for me wondering what was taking so long. When he spotted me struggling to fend off the attacks with an armful of books, I thought dad would make that punk leave me alone.

Instead, he grabbed the stack of books from my hand and told me to turn around and fight back. I don't know who was surprised more by his instructions, me or my assailant. Regardless, I followed dad's advice turning around to face this kid toe to toe. In case you think my dad's words might have erased the fear I was feeling you'd be mistaken. But it did inspire me to stand up for myself anyway, knowing I would probably get my butt kicked. The fight itself lasted only a few moments, as we moved around the schoolyard throwing punches back and forth. I guess one of the other kids ran and told on us because it wasn't long before the principal came running outside to break it up. He grabbed us both by the arm and was about to take us back to the office for disciplinary action when my dad stopped him. He said, "I'll take care of this one," as he took me by the hand leading me outside the gate and off the property.

We didn't talk much on the car ride home. As soon as we got to the house dad wanted me to tell my mother what happened at school. But since I was in no mood to talk he provided her with every last detail. It was like he was proud of me or something. Judging by the level of enthusiasm in his voice, I guess he was proud that I stuck up for myself. "Son," he said, "If you hadn't fought back he would have continued pushing you around all year long." All I could think about was how my first experience with fighting was as bad as I'd ever imagined. And now that I'd provoked him, I was certain that kid would be even madder the next day. That's when I informed my parents of my plan. I was never going back to school again. Then dad said, "I've dealt with plenty of bullies and believe me, after you stand up to them once they don't want to mess with you anymore. You're no longer an easy target." So he drove me to school the next day confident that my problem had been solved. What he said did seem to make sense, but I was still scared since it was my butt that was on the line. Thankfully, dad turned out to be right. Whenever I saw that kid again he always walked cautiously on the other side of the sidewalk, taking care not to even make eye contact with me.

When I didn't have my hands full laying down the law at school, somehow I managed to find enough time to manhandle my younger brother. Actually, we didn't fight as much as I may have led you to believe. The truth of the matter is that for a while we were each others only playmate. And when we fought, there was no one to play with which could get to be pretty boring. As a result, we tried to keep the confrontations to a minimum. At least until we got old enough to make other friends. That's when the chaos really started. Mom had a devil of a time keeping us in line, attempting to find creative methods of punishment that might actually have an impact on our unruly behavior. Her efforts were usually spent in vain and we seemed to kick it up a notch with every passing year. Kevin claims he has memories of being pinned to the ground, me hovering over top of him while spitting in his face. I think he's blowing things out of proportion with the whole face-spitting thing. He's probably still trying to get my parent's sympathy. However, I do seem to remember him having a strong aversion to being held down against his will. His fear was my fascination. I vividly recall the terrified look on his face as he struggled furiously to regain his freedom. It's amazing what a person can accomplish when they want something bad enough. Even though I was much bigger, he managed to wrestle his way out from under me nearly every time before my parents were able to intervene.

If you're thinking now that maybe I deserved what I got from that punk kid at school you're probably right. The abuse dished out to Kevin by my hands might even be misconstrued as bullying by some of you. Don't worry about him though, he would have his revenge. He figured out real quick that whenever I bothered him, a simple blood curdling squeal was enough to make my parents come running. And because he was smaller than me they inevitably placed the blame on my shoulders without fail. I'll admit that those first few years I deserved most of the punishment I received. But in time, Kevin got good at this game and started provoking me into fighting with him. Then he'd scream and my parents would respond. And even though he was lying about who instigated the fight, I still got the bulk of the responsibility for what happened. It seems mom and dad felt like I should know better since I was the oldest. Big deal, it wasn't like Kevin didn't know what he was doing. But he sure had the wool pulled over their eyes.

It was also during elementary school that I got my first taste of playing baseball. After expressing an interest in the sport (not to mention keeping Kevin and I separated), my parents signed me up to play the very next season. It was a total disaster. Watching the first game from the bleachers they observed me doing everything under the sun except playing baseball. I would play in the outfield dirt or stare off aimlessly into space, never paying much attention to the actual game itself. When our team finally came off the field my father told me I had a decision to make. He said that even though I was playing right field (a position often reserved for the worst player on the team in little league) my contribution was still important to the team. Besides, there was no sense in playing if I wasn't going to give a hundred percent. Anything worth doing is worth doing well. If I stepped back onto that baseball diamond it would be because I wanted to play ball. Otherwise, I could quit the team altogether and never go back. But dad wouldn't let me straddle the fence. I got the message loud and clear. From that day forward the game of baseball took on a whole new meaning for me, eventually becoming one of my greatest passions in life.

Finishing my last year of grade school, it was now time to move into the local sixth grade center. Most areas have three main divisions in the public education system. Elementary, middle, and high school seem to be the de facto standard in many cities across the country. Our system was somewhat different though, as there was a separate campus for both the sixth and the seventh grades. Then we got shipped off for the next two years to yet another location. And finally, we finished out the remaining three years of our academic career at the local high school.

Interestingly, the sixth grade center I attended had the unfortunate distinction of being the site of a young girl's kidnapping just a few years earlier. Tragedy struck our small town when Ted Bundy, the notorious serial killer, captured and later killed this innocent victim. No one knows for sure how he managed to lure her away from classmates and into his car. My parents, who were acquainted with her father, said he existed in a zombie like state after the death of his daughter was confirmed. As for Bundy, he was eventually caught and executed, but not before murdering again. When the date of his electrocution finally arrived it was met with a crowd of onlookers anxious to witness his demise. Their hatred for this man ran to the bone as they celebrated outside the state penitentiary. It became known by some as the "Bundy Barbecue" but most people were just glad it was over. It was kind of eerie going to school there knowing what had taken place on that very campus. None of the teachers ever mentioned a word but the students were abuzz with gossip the first week or two of classes. It didn't last long though, and after a couple of months passed things seemed to be getting back to normal. Or at least as normal as junior high school can be.

It was in sixth grade that I first became aware of how some kids were considered "cool" and others were not. Name brand clothing was becoming an important issue and I begged my mom for three weeks to buy me a pair of *Reebok* shoes. She finally caved in, but only after I convinced her of what a tremendous bargain they were compared to the cheap ones we'd been getting from K-mart. Nothing against the quality footwear carried by the national discounter, but these shoes were crafted from real leather and would take much longer for me to wear out. I reasoned that by getting me those stylish new kicks she would actually be saving money in the long run. The trick to getting what you want from my mother is in knowing how to speak her language. She wasn't completely naïve though, and what I didn't realize was *how much* longer that first pair of *Reeboks* would last. I put those things to the test as she wouldn't buy me another pair for almost an entire year. And that was just for shoes. It was like pulling teeth trying to negotiate my way out of Wrangler blue jeans into the trendy Bugle Boys pants all my friends were wearing.

Now it's not quite true that all my friends were really dressed in the latest styles. Most of them were having the same discussions with their own parents, attempting to persuade them into action. Whether it was superior negotiation skills on my part, or mom's strong sense of sympathy, my efforts finally paid off. Armed with a stylish wardrobe, I felt confident meeting new kids in school. It's amazing how wearing nice clothes can impact your level of effectiveness. But she wouldn't budge an inch on my idea for a new haircut. Many of my friends were trying out new fads in hair design and I wanted desperately to participate along with them. Of course some of the kids had mullets, a standard redneck hairstyle keeping it short up top while growing the back out much longer. But that style had become so common it was no longer on the edge of high fashion. These days the kids had turned their attention to a brand new hairdo that was sweeping the nation. This radical new fad was called a "rattail" and was every bit as sophisticated as the name implies. Based loosely on the formerly popular mullet type hairstyle, the rattail also utilized long hair growing down the back of the neck. But unlike its predecessor, only a few strands in the middle were grown long to imitate the look of a rat's tail extending from underneath an otherwise ordinary haircut. What a cool idea! Unfortunately mom refused to ever allow me to get one stating, "I will not have my son wearing a hairstyle named after a dirty little rodent." It didn't matter to her that my friends had already trimmed their mullets into this hot new style. There would be no further discussion, her decision was final.

By now Poco and I were best friends and we'd picked up a couple other stragglers along the way. One kid that always hung around was named Minnow. I'm not kidding, that was his real given birth name. It's no wonder he had trouble making friends with a name like that. Sometimes I can't help but wonder what in the hell these parents are thinking when they name their children. Don't they know how mean other kids can be? I'm not saying their behavior is right, but it happens all the time. Didn't they ever go to junior high? Anyway, we accepted Minnow despite his unique name. Already being friends with a guy named Poco I was in no position to pass judgment on anyone.

Another guy I became friends with was a boy named Bryan. He fit in pretty well with the group and we started hanging out at each other's houses. He had the best rope swing hanging from the branch of a giant oak tree in his front yard. The rope stretched near the ground where it passed through a hole that had been cut from the center of a small wooden board. It was tied off tight underneath, the piece of wood serving as a seat to ride upon. That thing was more fun than you can imagine, especially when his parents were away. Occasionally, mom would let me out of the house before my homework was finished. I'd jump on my bike and high tail it over to Bryan's as fast as possible, sometimes managing to make it there before his folks got home from work.

Those were the days we drug the rope swing up to the top of his parent's outdoor workshop and jumped off from there. Believe it or not I was a little bit timid the first time around. I had been burned by heights before and was in no hurry whatsoever to relive the experience of falling. Bryan reassured me by sharing the fact that he'd already done it hundreds of times before. Trusting my friend's advice, and seeking the thrill of a lifetime, I held on tight and leapt into the air. My legs wrapped themselves around the rope as my butt found the wooden seat. The ground was a total blur as my body whizzed past. What a rush. We took turns riding that swing until we heard his mom's car pull up out front. Then it was game over until next time.

4

"Boys will be Boys"

Growing up without a structured environment often leads directly to mischief. Even if we'd had more discipline I doubt it would've made much of a difference. After all, both parents were pretty hard on us when they caught us screwing up, but it never deterred us much from misbehaving in the future. We were always looking for trouble and we usually found it. The neighborhood we lived in was rather small and there wasn't much traffic on those back roads. Bikes were our preferred method of transport, allowing us to explore a sense of freedom and liberation we'd never experienced before.

One of our best friends as kids was a boy named Daryl who lived just across the street. Not the house with all the chicken coops that sat directly across from ours. The kid who lived there was much older and really mean, always threatening to beat us up whenever we rode down his street. He seemed to enjoy bullying us around. There was rumor about him having metal pins in both knees though, so we knew his Achilles heel if he were to ever make good on his threats.

Daryl lived on the other corner next to the same dirt road that ran beside our house. He was always a great friend to both me and Kevin. He was right between us in age and, because of his laid back demeanor, was able to get along pretty well with both of us. One thing I'll always remember is when he got his first Nintendo. We'd been spending all our money on video games down the street at the local gas station. Mario *Bros.* was a huge hit and I just couldn't get enough of that game. Once he got it for his new game system we spent most of our time playing over at his house. That's where we got our first taste of rap music.

Dee (as he now preferred to be called) had taken quite an interest in this unique genre of music. He bought all the popular cassettes, L.L. Cool Jay, Fat Boys, and Run DMC as soon as they hit the record store shelves. His mom even got him one of those boom boxes with the big speakers so he could carry it around on his shoulder. It's odd but I don't remember him taking it out of his house except on a couple occasions. Maybe it was too heavy for him since the darn thing was nearly half his size. Or it could've been the six size D batteries it required for a couple short hours of play time proved too big an expense. At any rate it was the greatest thing to sit around his house playing Nintendo while listening to his growing tape collection.

One day he looked over at me and said, "Hey, you want to hear something cool?" Of course I was always up for being cool so naturally I said, "Sure!" He reached way back into his sock drawer and retrieved a tape I'd never seen before. Right away I noticed the "Parental Guidance" sticker on the front meaning no one over eighteen could buy it. "Where did you get that?" I asked, waiting anxiously for what I was about to hear. Mom had taken great care to instill a strong sense of morals into both her children. This represented the first time those values would be tested in her absence.

When the music finally started I tried my best to maintain my composure. I didn't want "Dee" to think I wasn't cool, but at the same time I knew what I was hearing was wrong, especially with Kevin sitting right there beside me. As much as we fought over the years, I was still his big brother and felt a strong obligation to look out for him. After the first couple songs I'd had enough and told our host we had to get home for dinner. I think he knew the music made me a little uncomfortable because he never played it again when we were around.

It wasn't long before we'd beaten *Mario Bros.* many times. We found all the secret worlds, got infinite free men, and jumped over the flag pole. What was once the hottest thing around faded quickly into obscurity as there was nothing left to accomplish. So we began spending more of our time outdoors. It was during this time that both Daryl and I developed a love for the game of baseball. Every day it wasn't raining you could find us in my backyard tossing around the ball. Whenever we could round up a couple friends, we'd take live pitching or play home run derby.

Not all the kids in the neighborhood were as great a friend as Daryl. For instance, there was this one little punk living two doors down from us that was always getting me into trouble. He wasn't very nice and hated it when he didn't get his way. But sometimes he was the only choice available. It was either hang out with him or do nothing at all. The times I found myself playing with Josh usually ended in regret.

For example, the worst whipping I ever got in my life was thanks to that kid. A few of us were playing in my yard when Josh suggested we go over to his house for some snacks. His parents were sleeping and he said we could have all the sodas and candy bars we could handle. Getting to pig out on junk food was as appealing to me as any kid that age, but insisted I needed to get permission from my folks first. That got me a lot of ribbing from the guys about having to ask if I could leave the yard. It was Josh's taunting in particular that finally pushed me into going without letting my dad know about it. This turned out to be one of the biggest errors in judgment of my entire childhood. He eventually came looking for me and when he found me there was hell to pay. Standing in Josh's open doorway he discovered me sitting inside their kitchen helping myself to a variety of his parent's junk food. To say he was angry is a bit of an understatement. He was furious. Walking inside, he jerked me out of that chair and yanked off his belt. Then he pushed me out of the house, whipping me the moment we stepped outside.

He had a knack for striking us right across the upper thigh where he knew it would sting the most. I brought that on myself though when I stuffed an Archie comic book down the back of my pants, knowing full well a spanking was on the way. It might have worked too, if not for me grinning ear to ear just a few moments after the whipping. Dad figured out real quick that we'd pulled a fast one on him and he was livid. We really got it good that day.

After disobeying a direct order not to leave the front yard, I had my father in a panic wondering where I'd gone. Mom was scared half to death which didn't help defuse the situation. He took that belt to my backside all the way down Josh's steps, through his front yard and into the street. The punishment continued all the way down the road, through our chain link fence, up the front steps and into the house. In fact, he didn't let up until I reached my room. Talk about having a bad day. All because I was dumb enough to listen to that punk when it went against my better judgment.

Josh's parents weren't very tough on him in the area of discipline. But with an ex drill instructor for a father you can bet that Kevin and I got our fair share. As dad put it, "Son, when I was in the Corps men had to do what I said, when I said it. Their life and the lives of other young men depended on it." I think he had a tiny bit of trouble readjusting to civilian life. Part of my mistake was reminding him of that fact. When he would spout off about saving lives I'd say something like, "So how is me not cleaning my room going to save anybody's life?" He didn't find my sarcastic remarks nearly as funny as I did.

As tough as dad was on us boys, my mother could be just as bad. She had her own methods of discipline that were equally effective. One of the ways mom used to keep us in line was washing our mouths out with soap. The first time it happened was because of that same kid Josh. Well, it was really more my own fault, but he did provoke me. We were both walking along the concrete walkway right outside my mom's bedroom window. He'd picked up this nasty habit of cursing and was calling me every name in the book. I think he was trying to show off by using any profanity he could think of. Finally I'd had about enough and began shouting a slew of obscenities right back at him. I rattled off so many off-color four letter words it made his head spin. Apparently, it made my mother's head spin around too. Right toward her open window. She was lying in on her bed and heard every single word I said. "Wesley Brent Basham, get in her right now!" she shouted, as I headed inside to face the music.

Believe me, if you've never had the wonderful taste of soap in your mouth you aren't missing much. It's horrible. Actually, it really depends a great deal on the kind of soap that's being used. Some of them aren't all that bad, comparatively speaking. But there are a couple brands that I swear must've been specifically tested for this purpose. Some of these products are so intolerable I bet the manufacturers could even market them that way. "Want to get rid of your child's dirty mouth? Wash it clean with *Brand X*, hated by more children in national taste tests!"

Without the benefits of informative ads like these, my mother was relegated to using whatever brand was most handy. She frequently bought Zest to use in the shower so it was always ready at a moment's notice. Sometimes she would get the cheap stuff and there really is a big difference. The generic brands just don't pack much of a punch. But Zest is pretty powerful stuff. One advantage we found with that particular brand was that it's pretty easy to get off with a minimal amount of scrubbing.

I think mom felt bad the first few times she used such a barbaric method of discipline. It wore off pretty fast though and she soon began making us put our tongue back inside our mouth and close it down tight. Then she'd make us stand there a minute or two to make sure the punishment had the desired affect. That's when it became a battle of wills. What she didn't know was that we figured out how to stop most of the taste. The trick is to keep the sides of your tongue from touching any area of your mouth before you get the chance to rinse it out.

There was one day when we'd smarted off to her and she couldn't find the Zest. What a lucky coincidence for us, there were no bars of soap to be found anywhere in the house. Every bit of it had curiously disappeared. Even the spare bars she kept stored away in the bathroom closet were gone. It was as though burglars had broken into our home stealing every bar of soap we owned. Kevin and I sat smugly while my mother grew angrier by the minute. All of a sudden she stopped dead in her tracks and headed straight for the kitchen. It seems we forgot all about the dish soap she kept underneath the kitchen sink.

She returned to her room where we were still awaiting punishment and told us both to open wide. In her right hand was a bottle of Lux dishwashing soap. The top was open and the thick pink liquid was seeping out around the edges. I was not looking forward to this. "Stick out your tongue," she barked as we nervously complied with her request. When that first drop of soap hit the tip of my tongue it was all over. It penetrated every taste bud instantly. There wasn't another brand around that could compare to such a horrible taste. It was that bad believe me, because by this time I had become quite the expert on the subject. Seeing our reaction to just a couple drops of this toxic stuff made mom realize the fun and games were over, she'd finally gained the upper hand.

Lest you think my mom was physically abusive to us as kids, let me assure you that we were the ones who pushed her into such drastic measures. We were defiant, sneaky, manipulative, and nothing she tried would deter us from misbehaving. Besides, I think we've moved past the statute of limitations for her actions and if provoked there's no doubt she can still get her hands on a bottle of Lux in a pinch. Sometimes it's better not to rock the boat. She was at her wits end when she discovered the soap idea. It was quite effective, especially when used to combat our sarcastic attitudes. And even if we did still get into trouble, at least now we tried extra hard not to get caught.

Of all my friends Poco was probably the most unique. As I mentioned earlier, we met in the first grade and became friends right away. The local fire department visited our school that year and getting sprayed down by a giant fire hose turned out to be quite the bonding experience. It seemed like every weekend we were hanging out at each other's house. He came to be pretty good friends with Daryl as well, visiting the neighborhood so often. With a peculiar name like Poco, he got his share of ribbing from the other boys. It usually didn't go too far though as he had a friendly, almost disarming quality about him that you couldn't help but appreciate. Other kids, including myself, were naturally drawn to his charismatic personality. Hanging around with him almost guaranteed you of having a good time.

His grandfather owned a cabinet shop in town and even sponsored a little league baseball team one year. His dad served as head coach, picking me to play on their team. Of all the years I played baseball this was definitely the most fun. For one thing, Poco and I got to play on the same team. He wasn't really into the sport, but because of his father's love for the game, he gave it his best shot. The other reason I enjoyed playing for Eddie was his unique style of coaching. On the one hand he took his job very seriously, expecting us to give it our all on the playing field. On the other, he always had fun out there and was never afraid to attempt trick plays to fool the other team. Like having me square around to bunt causing the infield to charge home plate, only to pull back at the last second, smashing the ball down the third base line. Or the time we faked stealing second base. With two men on and down by a run, it was time to execute our plan. I took off from first with the pitch, acting like I didn't realize somebody was already on second. He instructed me to stay put as I stopped halfway down the baseline, pretending to suddenly realize my mistake. Looking frantic I turned around to run back toward first. By this time the catcher was completely confused and ended up throwing the ball over the first baseman's head. Eddie was ecstatic as he watched the play unfold exactly the way he'd imagined. Yep, playing baseball with Poco and his father was highly entertaining.

The cabinet shop itself did quite well supplying custom built cabinets to much of the surrounding area. As a result of its success, their family was able to enjoy a very affluent lifestyle. Growing up, Poco always had the latest and greatest toys on the market. Not to mention the trampoline, go karts, and multiple motorized vehicles given to him as gifts from his grandparents. He never wanted for anything. And yet there were times he seemed so unhappy. Aside from spoiling the grandchildren, Poco's grandfather put his money to good use like sponsoring a car at the local race track. We got into the races for free and were sometimes even allowed down in the pit with the driver. But racing wasn't the only thing his grandfather sank his money into.

He also owned his very own hunting club. A few miles of wilderness belonged to him and all the members were granted access to his private acreage. They hunted for almost anything but focused primarily on shooting deer. As Poco and I grew older, they shifted away from using rifles into using a more difficult weapon, the compound bow. His dad used to spend hours in the tree stand waiting quietly for a big buck to pass underneath. Of course sitting in one spot all day could get pretty boring and it wasn't long before they abandoned this technique altogether. Besides, it was hard enough climbing up into the tree carrying a twelve pack of beer under one arm. And getting down after drinking all twelve was next to impossible. A few broken bones and one dislocated shoulder was enough to put an end to that nonsense.

That's when they discovered the beauty of hunting with dogs. It was too good to be true. Just turn the beagles loose in the woods and they'd bring the deer out to you. I remember sitting in the truck on the side of the road while Poco's dad downed a few cans of Coors, waiting patiently for his prey to arrive. Sure enough, as the barking continued to draw closer, the deer would dart across the road only a few yards away. They'd gone back to using modern weaponry by this point and bagged plenty of trophies along the way. It was like shooting fish in a barrel, whatever that means. If they shot and missed though, the guys had some kind of strange ceremony back at the lodge, pinning the shirt tale of the inductee onto their infamous *Wall of Shame*. But most of the guys were pretty good with a gun even when they were HUI (hunting under the influence), and there was always plenty of fresh venison for everyone to enjoy.

Because Poco lived so far out in the sticks, the only way we could play together was to get one of our parents to drive. And we still needed an adult present to supervise. So most of the time we got to play together out was on the weekends. During the school week my friend Bryan and I began spending more time hanging out since he lived only a short bike ride away. One afternoon he began telling me about his wonderful experience at summer camp the previous year. It sounded amazing. Bryan's enthusiasm was contagious and pretty soon I wanted to go too. He didn't see any reason why not and we invited Poco along as well. What a fantastic idea. The only thing that sounded better than going off to camp was getting to go with two of your closest friends. Now if we could only convince our parents, we'd be in business.

Both Poco and I realized that if either one of us could get permission to go with Bryan, it would become much easier to get the other parents to follow suit. So we set out on our mission. Out of the field of possible candidates, it was Poco's mom who appeared easiest to break. Both our dads took a strict disciplinary role in the family and were ruled out immediately. That left us with only two choices. Deciding which mother we would target was a no-brainer since mine had mostly grown wise to my tricks. Once Poco convinced his mom to let him go, a simple phone call was all it took to seal the deal for me too. They would also take care of breaking the news to our fathers. Looking back, I realize our parents didn't stand a chance. We were absolutely determined to go to summer camp that year. After listening to Bryan's description of his most recent trip, nothing short of dying would've kept us away.

The anticipation and excitement peaked as we arrived at Camp Kulaqua. Poco's mom had been kind enough to drive us to the location of our week long adventure. Waving goodbye, we sensed a great time ahead and knew we wouldn't be disappointed. Bryan had already been dropped off and was waiting eagerly for us to join him. When he found us, he was speaking nearly ninety miles an hour and I thought he might burst from all the excitement. The camp was nestled quietly back in the wilderness providing the perfect backdrop for the exciting activities ahead.

The one thing Bryan hadn't bothered to mention was that this was a church affiliated camp. Being raised as Christians, this didn't bother either one of us in the least. That is until we sat down to eat that night at dinner. The first clue that something was amiss came while standing in line waiting for our food. It was served cafeteria style and that evening's offering was hamburgers and fries. Up to this point everything seemed alright until I attempted to pour some ketchup on my burger. Getting a closer look at the meat I noticed it looked very peculiar, like nothing I'd ever seen before. About the same time I could tell by the perplexed look on Poco's face that he was noticing the same thing. That's when it dawned on us. These weren't regular all beef hamburgers at all. They were the artificial type made mostly of soy. And the reason they were serving soy burgers was because this particular religious denomination happened to be vegetarian. In all the time I'd known Bryan he never bothered to mention a word of this to either of us. Nor did he think it might be relevant to bring up when inviting us to camp. Now we were going to have to go without eating real meat for an entire week! It was almost too much to bear. In my house, not a meal went by that I didn't have some kind of dead animal on my plate. We even hunted our own food for goodness sake. I attempted to call my mom three times that first night to convince her to come take me home. But Bryan insisted it wouldn't be that bad. Tomorrow would come soon and that's when the fun would crank into high gear. Against my better judgment I put down the phone and got ready for bed.

Waking bright and early to the sound of an over zealous youth counselor shouting "Rise and shine ladies, time to get up," was not my idea of starting the morning off on the right foot. But since this was only the first day of camp with a full week left to go, I thought better of making waves. Not yet anyway. Like it or not, this creampuff was in a temporary position of power and could easily make my life a living hell. So I played along with his little game. At least while he was around. Whenever he took off to flirt with the female counselors, which was quite often, we were left unsupervised in our cabin for hours on end. It was party time. Screaming profanities at each other, freestyle wrestling matches, and blaring rock music on our appointed supervisor's boom-box were among our favorite ways of expressing ourselves. We were pre-adolescent young boys. Rebelling against authority figures was a basic rite of passage.

Eventually our misbehavior got out of hand. One of the guys, Alex, told us he knew how to make somebody pass out using only his bare hands. There was no way we were going to believe him unless he was willing to demonstrate. He was reluctant at first, but with enough poking we were able to persuade him. Grabbing a "volunteer", they stood him firmly against the wall. We decided it best to have someone hold each of his arms just in case it actually worked. No one wanted to see the kid get hurt or anything. That would be irresponsible. Standing there in anticipation, he was instructed to take three deep breaths holding the last one in without exhaling. As soon as solid pressure was applied to the right spot, his whole body instantly became dead weight. His eyes rolled back in his head and he dropped like a rock. It was all the spotters could do to keep his head from slamming against the floor. Everyone stood there in silent disbelief staring at the lifeless body lying before us. Breaking the silence Poco exclaimed, "That was the coolest thing I've ever seen!" And it was. But as the seconds slowly ticked away, we began to wonder if this kid was still alive. Talk about an adrenaline rush. One guy checked for a pulse and gave us the thumbs up. Slapping our comatose victim across the face a few times did the trick as he began to regain consciousness. We'd seen enough as this was plenty of excitement for one day.

The activities provided by the camp proved even more dangerous than the trouble we found by ourselves. Each morning at breakfast we got to select which excursion we'd like to participate in later that day. Signup sheets filled up fast, each cabin taking turns choosing their favorite activities. Horseback riding, canoeing, tubing, and four wheeling were among the most popular. If your cabin was one of the last to pick that day you could forget about getting any of these. I was fortunate enough to try them all at least once.

I managed to go tubing twice, trading a kid some beef jerky mom sent me in the mail for his spot. What he didn't realize was there was a food cart located conveniently at the end of our river ride. After a week without meat, the smell of hot dogs and sausages was like pure heaven. But the first time we went I didn't bring any money along. It was like pure torture having to watch a couple of the other kids eat in front of me. You may wonder how they thought to bring cash along. Well it turns out they already knew of the cart's existence. But they also understood that if word got out too fast the gig would be up and their chances of coming back again would be nil. They even went so far as sharing a small piece of food with the rest of us in order to keep our mouths shut. And it worked too. We didn't tell a soul about our experience. If anyone asked we'd tell them that the river was incredibly cold (which was true) and the ride was really rather boring (also true). We just left out the other details and let them draw their own conclusion.

Two of the activities turned out to be extremely hazardous to my health. When I chose horseback riding it was due to a lack of alternatives. Coming close to just hanging out in the cabin and reading most of the day, I changed my mind at the last minute. Turns out I'd live to regret it. We met at the stables and chose the horse we wanted to ride. Most of the others had some experience with those imposing animals. Not me. And it didn't take long for something terrible to happen. Riding along a small wilderness trail we came upon a small obstacle. A rather large tree had fallen recently blocking our path through the woods. The other horses had no trouble at all, simply hopping over it and continuing on their journey. My horse was different. He stopped dead in his tracks refusing to move an inch. At the instruction of my counselor I encouraged him to jump by lightly smacking him on the behind. This was not the best move as he turned to the side and darted out into the heavy brush beside the trail. Apparently, my actions spooked the creature causing him to sprint through the woods full speed ahead. Tree branches whacked me across the face and I saw my entire life flash before my eyes. When someone finally caught up with us they offered me a ride back into camp. "No offense," I said, "But I'd rather walk instead."

After an experience like that, who would've thought it could get any worse? Well it did the day we got to hot rod around on four wheelers. These all terrain vehicles (ATV's) were tuned up and ready to ride as we set out for the track running just outside of camp. All the engines were outfitted with a governor, limiting them to a certain speed in the interest of better safety. My particular ATV must've been geared lower than the other machines because it didn't take long for me to fall behind the rest of the pack. Even though I was going full throttle, I was gradually falling further and further behind. They disappeared behind a cloud of dirt which was, incidentally, the very same cloud that caused my accident. Heading full speed into their wake, the dust hit my eyes causing immediate blindness. Now would have probably been a good time to let up on the accelerator but the thought never entered my mind. Instead I kept cruising along, off the dirt pathway straight into a barbed wire fence. It seems that my innate talent for getting hurt followed me all the way to summer camp.

As the week drew to a close the counselors wanted to do something fun for us on our last day. They decided upon a *Gong Show* inspired talent contest for our final evening together. It turned out to be very entertaining with one act stealing the show. Earlier in the week, on one of the tubing excursions, a young girl got bit by a potentially rabid otter. Apparently, she was trying to pet this "adorable" creature when it turned and attacked her. The only wound she suffered was a minor bite on the arm. If you've ever seen an otter you know that they aren't the most ferocious creature in the animal kingdom. Nor are they very aggressive. More than likely, the girl simply got too close, and it was probably just trying to protect its young. Still though, the camp nurse felt it best to give her a shot just in case the otter had rabies. If it were rabid, that would explain the aggressive behavior. Either way, it was better not to take any chances. Unfortunately, the shot had to be administered right in her rear end. There was quite a buzz going around camp about the mishap. All the kids were talking about it, a few of them reenacting the event for the talent show. One of them dragged an inner tube on stage and sat inside. Another, dressed in a full body otter costume, ran out and attacked his victim. That poor girl had to sit there watching those goofballs mock her misery on stage for everyone to see. At least it would all be over soon.

5

"Family Tradition"

This wouldn't be much of a redneck book without including a healthy dose of extended family. And we have plenty to go around. So much in fact, that if you ever want to borrow one of them I'm sure something can be arranged. Heck, take anybody you want, I'll even give you the pick of the litter. Oh, and don't worry about getting them back home too quickly. Take all the time you need getting acquainted, I'm sure they'll overstay their welcome soon enough.

I've already mentioned both parents and my younger brother Kevin. But there are other members of the family in desperate need of an introduction. Take my two cousins John and Matt (or Moose as he would later be known) for example. The force is strong in these two. There is enough redneck blood coursing through their veins to give the entire state of Alabama a complete transfusion if necessary. Which is probably why they fit in with Kevin and I as well as they did. We're all cut from the very same cloth. The sad reality is that nobody ever bothered to break the mold after we were born. Actually, one could make a strong argument that the mold was already broken before our die had ever been cast. And as far as I know, we are all still legally allowed to procreate. I personally believe there should be some kind of law, protecting the general public from this sort of thing. Rednecks begetting rednecks has caused more than enough trouble in this country already. But as it sits now, the four of us are free to release our offspring into an unsuspecting world, destined to wreak havoc upon society for generations to come.

Calling John and Matt our cousins doesn't provide the most accurate depiction of our relationship with them. They were really more like brothers than anything else. After some complications at home the boys came to live at our house for a while. We built forts, rode dirt bikes, and even forged creeks in search of crawfish together. Hanging out with each other so frequently naturally led to a certain amount of conflict. Fighting is inevitable when grouping four young boys together for a prolonged period of time. It's nothing to be concerned about.

Sometimes you just have to let them work it out amongst themselves. Of the four of us, John and I were the least likely to back down. Maybe it was because we were the oldest but whatever the reason, there's no doubt that one hell of a stubborn streak ran through us both. This unwillingness to resist confrontation was probably the same character trait that kept me in constant hot water with my mother. When it came to a test of wills she won the battle every single time. Being a kid, there was only so much I could do when things became heated between us. And she always had an ace or two up her sleeve if she ever felt the balance of power shifting in my direction. "Go to your room" or "You just wait until your father gets home" were usually sufficient to put an end to the conflict. But with John, it was different. He was more my peer, and with no clear advantage for either of us our arguments could easily last for hours on end. It would start out innocently enough. First there was a disagreement of opinion followed closely by a heated debate. This usually moved directly into a screaming match, one we believed would be won by whoever was able to yell the loudest. For some reason, drowning out the sound of John's voice reinforced my belief that he was wrong. From there it typically evolved into a knock down drag out wrestling match, the loser becoming even angrier than before. It seems that kicking the crap out of someone isn't the best way to win them over to your way of thinking.

I don't mean to give you the impression that we fought all the time. Actually, it was exactly the opposite. Most of the time we spent together found us getting along terrifically. But when we did get into it sparks really flew. Kevin and Matt were relegated to damage control trying their best to calm us down. They knew that our fighting would cause the parents to get involved and the fun would be over. So they did their best to diffuse the situation if it arose. Especially Matt, he was the most even tempered young boy I've ever known. Almost always in control of his temper I've only seen him lose control once in his life. And what a site it was.

Because of his easygoing nature, John made a habit of getting amusement from picking on the poor guy. He tolerated years of abuse until one day he finally snapped. Playing in their front yard John was poking and prodding his younger brother, doing anything he could to get a rise out of him. You should have seen his face when Matt turned to face his attacker. He shouted, "Enough!" as he reached for the broken shovel handle lying on the ground. Sensing the fury in Matt's eyes I think John would have run for his life if he hadn't been paralyzed with shock. After all, he'd been teasing his brother for years and he'd never retaliated before. I guess this was the straw that broke the camel's back and he headed straight for John. Slamming the wooden rod down across his back he exclaimed,

"I'm tired of you bothering me all the time. Leave me alone!" I think he got the message loud and clear this time as Matt got his revenge. The bruises from that fateful day lasted over two weeks and John gained a newfound respect for his little brother.

My own altercations with John stemmed from our growing fascination with playing board games. His insatiable interest in military strategy kept him preoccupied with defeating me on the chose field of battle. We logged in many hours of game play, constantly seeking a way to get an edge on our opponent. The fact of the matter is John was flat out better than me. He thought like a real live general and the more complex the game, the less chance I had for victory. Playing games like *Stratego* and *Risk*, we were pretty evenly matched and the game could usually go either way. But when we upped the ante and started playing *Axis and Allies* my luck quickly ran out.

Based on World War II, this game featured multiple pieces each with their own strengths. There were infantry men, armored tanks, long range bombers, and fighter planes (like the Japenese Zero's) to name a few. Compared to only two different pieces on the *Risk* board, it required a great deal more focus and a better strategy of attack. John used the increased complexity to pick me apart one piece at a time. Beating me was child's play for him leaving me disheartened and extremely frustrated. After getting my butt handed to me the first few times we played I decided to try a new tactic. John was still focused on beating me at *Axis and Allies* while I turned my attention to a new game. Realizing the futility of trying to beat him on the game board, I took the liberty of moving the contest inside John's head. This new game was called "See how long it takes to piss John off," and the odds were once again stacked in my favor. And I must say it was amazingly easy to exploit his weakness. Every time we played there came point when we both knew the game was over. There was nothing left to do but play out the remaining moves. Now when we reached that point I pushed my chair back from the table and calmly stated "I quit". Being so close to victory only to have me walk away infuriated him. He insisted we continue saying "You can't quit, the game's not over yet". "It's over," I replied. "We both know you're going to win." But he wanted to keep going. He knew that unless we completed the game, there would always be a small element of doubt about who would've won if we'd kept playing. He also knew I'd be sure to remind him of that at a later date. The more I refused the angrier he got. That was more like it, finally a game I could enjoy. After a while, John caught on to my little game and then he was the one who refused to play. But it sure was fun while it lasted.

The guys lived near the edge of town on the other side of the railroad tracks. My grandmother bought two trailers, one for the kids and their parents and the other for her. She put them both on the same piece of property and took an active interest in raising the two young boys. They spent so much time with her that she eventually became the central authority figure in their life. We didn't attend the same elementary school although we were all pretty close in age. John was the oldest, born just two years after me. Matt was a couple years younger than him, about the same age as Kevin. The common thread that connected us all was our knack for getting ourselves into trouble.

Out back of the property, behind both trailers, was a stretch of land covered with thick overgrowth. It was the perfect home for a variety of woodland creatures, some of which were even edible. We'd haul our BB guns out there trying our best to hunt down some wild game for dinner. Squirrels were the most abundant target, but not exactly at the top of my list of outdoor delicacies. It wasn't even on the list. I'd have rather eaten one of my mom's infamous turkey necks or chicken hearts. Sharing my distaste for these "tree rats", the guys and I focused instead on hunting quail or rabbits to feast upon.

Killing our prey was a piece of cake with the air powered BB gun Kevin got for Christmas. Is it me, or does his receiving a weapon for a present on Jesus' birthday seem strange to anyone else? Anyway, one afternoon John borrowed the gun to take some target practice out back. That's when he noticed a telephone repairman who was busy fixing the line next door. He was halfway up the ladder when John got him in his sights. To this day I don't understand what possessed him to take aim at another human being. But that's exactly what he did and as I've said before, John's quite the marksman. With his target squarely in sight, he gently squeezed the trigger sending a single pellet flying toward the ladder. As the bullet struck the man in the buttocks, he grabbed the wound out of instinct and promptly fell to the ground. John freaked out when he saw this and darted back inside. Apparently, he didn't think the gun had enough power to make it across both yards much less enough to penetrate the skin. It took him forever to talk his way out of that one.

There's no doubt of my family's inborn ability to get into mischief. But at least we got it honest. My grandmother shared many stories about the trouble our fathers got into when they were our age. She had enough tales of their misbehavior I could've written a prequel to this book, *The Redneck Chronicles: "Hereditary Insanity"*. Some people are simply predisposed toward certain unrefined character traits. In our case, the apple doesn't fall too far from the tree. So it was no surprise when John and Matt's dad managed to pull a fast one on us.

He convinced the four of us we could turn a nice profit selling what he called deer tongue tobacco. He said the Native Americans used it for years in lieu of regular tobacco because it was so plentiful and inexpensive. And wouldn't you know it, the stuff just happened to be scattered all over their front yard. All we had to do was gather the leaves together, setting them in a pile to dry. We couldn't believe our luck. The next two weeks found us collecting our treasure in John and Matt's front yard every day after school. We never did sell anything to the Native Americans their father had mentioned. Come to think of it, we didn't even know any Native Americans and ended up selling the whole lot of it to their dad for about five bucks. Pretty cheap labor if you ask me. Of course he could have just as easily made his boys do it for free. But why do that? Getting the yard clean and jerking our chain at the same time was far more entertaining.

Our relationship with the cousins from my mom's side of the family wasn't as tight as with John and Matt. Not because we didn't like them as much, it was simply a matter of geography. Both her sisters and their families lived a few hours away making it difficult to get together on a regular basis. Cherie, along with her husband and two daughters had moved into the growing metropolis of Atlanta, Georgia. Despite the physical distance between us, my parents made every effort to visit our relatives as often as possible.

Over the next couple years we embarked upon many family road trips, packing up the station wagon and heading north to the "hub of the south." This was perfectly fine with me for one simple reason, Braves games. My love of baseball was at its peak and traveling to Atlanta gave me a chance to catch the pros play live. And baseball wasn't the only thing they had to do up there. The city was growing at a torrid pace, due to a phenomenon commonly referred to as urban sprawl, resulting in a vast selection of activities for everyone to enjoy.

During one of our summer visits, Cherie took the liberty of planning an outdoor adventure floating down the Chattahoochie River. She found somewhere to rent the rafts and was surprisingly able to reserve two of them on very short notice. Spending the day white water rafting on the river during the hottest part of the year was incredibly appealing. That's why it seemed so peculiar that she was able to secure our spots so easily, and on a weekend no less. Those days were usually booked weeks in advance. But you wouldn't hear us complain. None of us had ever been on a rafting trip before and were looking forward to the opportunity. And what an experience it turned out to be.

Arriving in town late that evening, our excursion was scheduled for the following morning. I could barely sleep as images of braving wild rapids zipped through my mind. What if we lost our oars in the water? What if I got tossed overboard into the raging current? Would I be able to survive? How could I toss Kevin over-board and make it look like an accident? All the excitement was making me rest-less. After what seemed like hours of tossing and turning I finally passed out from exhaustion.

Upon opening my eyes the next day, the adrenaline kicked in and I bounced right to my feet. My mother was having some trouble waking Kevin so I volun-teered to help her out. Aware of my less than subtle methods of getting his atten-tion, she politely declined. Wise move on her part. Especially considering how bored I was that morning. Patience has never been my strong suit. But somehow I managed to survive without dying from boredom, waiting what seemed like for-ever for everyone to get the show on the road.

Arriving at the park, we picked up our rafts and headed down to the river. There was one spot designed specifically for launching the boats into the water. It was meant to provide easy access but you'd have never known that watching my family struggle to get started. Out of everyone, my father seemed to be having the most difficulty hopping aboard. The laws of gravity were having their way with him as he attempted to step out from the shoreline onto the raft. It pulled his body straight down into the water every time. He made three attempts before finally succeeding. It might have happened sooner if he'd asked for some help, but he refused to be given assistance from anyone. If he'd survived boot camp on Paris Island, he could certainly do this. Lucky for him, his oversized belly acted as the perfect floatation device and he floated right to the surface every time. If Mr. Darwin had been alive to witness this unlikely event it may have caused him to reconsider his famed theory of evolution (based on the survival of the fittest). But the real miracle that day was when he finally managed to navigate his way into the raft. After getting situated he helped the rest of us climb on board and shoved off from shore.

Call me crazy, but for all the anticipation this was turning out to be a pretty lame trip. With a lack of strong current the raft was hardly moving at all and there were no signs of white water rapids anywhere. My mom, however, was hav-ing a fabulous time cruising peacefully along the water's surface. She looked con-tent to bask in the sun and enjoy the ride. But I was getting restless. If the brochure promised the adventure of rough water then that's what should be delivered. We did hit a small ripple or two but nothing to get worked up about. I wanted more excitement, like the stuff I'd seen on television. Unfortunately, heavy action just wasn't in the cards for us this time, at least not in the way I expected.

Resigning myself to an uneventful day on the river, I settled back into the boat and tried to get comfortable. After all, it wasn't like I could go anywhere. Might as well try and make the best of it. Mom was enjoying herself just fine. Their generation always seemed to appreciate peace and quiet, maybe a little relaxation would do the trick for me as well. Dad appeared content just getting a chance to spend the day with family. Never in a million years could we have guessed what was waiting for us around the next bend.

I think it was my father who noticed it first. As we rounded the corner, the tree line began to disappear revealing a sight I'll never forget. Off in the distance, about fifty yards ahead of us, were hundreds of other rafts parked across the river near the sole rest stop along our journey. They were scattered everywhere covering the water from one side to the other as we were headed toward them. My dad wasn't much for crowds, especially when it came to us boys, but was left with no other choice. He quickly chose the path of least resistance and carefully guided the craft in that direction. Of course my suggestion to stop and use the restroom facilities was completely out of the question. "Just hang it over the side and quit complaining," he said, focusing intently on the task at hand.

Moving closer we noticed an extreme amount of partying going on in the boats ahead. They looked to be celebrating some kind of event as cheers and chants echoed their way across the water. All of a sudden my dad panicked. He began paddling furiously upriver in a futile attempt to escape. Wondering what could cause him to react so dramatically, I picked up my head to see for myself. I certainly got an eyeful. Finally close enough to make out their faces, these women were either extraordinarily hairy or they weren't women at all. Looking around I realized there weren't any girls anywhere. Oh there were plenty of bikinis, but they weren't being worn by females.

Come to find out, Atlanta is home to one of the largest gay populations in the entire United States. Not surprisingly, first place goes to the infamous San Francisco but the city of Atlanta ranks a strong second in queers per capita. And it seems they celebrate their gayness every year by spending the day rafting down the Chattahoochie River. No wonder it was so easy to get reservations, everyone else in their right mind was miles away from the river that day. But not us, there we were smack dab in the middle of all the festivities. If you could've only seen the look on my dad's face as he fought his way through the maze of rafts that fateful summer day, definitely not his first choice for a family vacation. I'm sure it wasn't exactly what Cherie expected either when she first planned the trip. Nevertheless, it became an experience none of us would ever forget.

Not all the family trips were as eventful as "The day the gays came out in Georgia" but it was always fun getting to visit with our cousins. Sometimes they'd come see us in Lake City too, but the bulk of the traveling was done by us. I can't imagine why they didn't drive down more frequently, especially with the wide range of activities our hometown had to offer. But for some reason that's the way it worked out and my parents logged many miles on that old wood paneled station wagon.

For a while, dad was making good money and it seemed like we saw them all the time. He'd apparently found his true calling selling tools from one of those mobile *Snap On* trucks. Renowned for their lifetime guarantee and rigid durability, the stuff he had onboard practically sold itself. Most of his regular customers were local mechanics. They were always looking to upgrade or add a few more pieces to their toolset. And the toolboxes he carried were also extremely popular with this segment of the market. They weren't inexpensive but were manufactured at a much higher quality than the competition. As a result, they bought exclusively from my father since the territory was guaranteed to him by the company. Financially, things were going very well for us as dad pulled down an annual income in the neighborhood of six figures. It wouldn't last long though and he sold the entire operation a couple years later.

During my lifetime I've witness that man come to the brink of success more than once only to pull the plug at the last minute. He attributes these occurrences to a debilitating condition known as survivor's guilt, imprinted upon his subconscious from his experiences in Vietnam. He claims that whenever he begins to feel successful about his life, he can't help but remember his buddies who didn't make it home alive. With every new success came feelings of remorse, constantly reminding him of the friends he left behind. Feeling guilty for living life at a higher level, he unwittingly sabotaged his own efforts at the expense of our family's financial well being. It's as though struggling to survive after the war ended kept him connected somehow to his fallen compatriots. But I believe they'd have preferred he live his life to the fullest, appreciating the little things while making the most of every moment he had left upon this earth. Heaven knows there are no second chances.

I'm no psychologist, but it's my opinion that this debilitating mental syndrome plaguing my father is only partially responsible for his actions. Based on careful observation, including much introspection of my own experiences, I feel there is something else lying at the root of the problem. It seems to me that he may actually be afraid of reaching the true success in life that he deserves. I'm not blaming my father at all because I know exactly how he feels. Coming from a redneck background like ours, the bar for success is sometimes set pretty low. It can be downright scary when attempting to stretch beyond the expectations of others. This phenomenon is not exclusive to my family either. Children often follow the path laid out by the previous generation, and though technically not a genetic trait, the results are often the same.

Whatever the reason for his behavior it had a dramatic impact on our family. Dad bounced around from job to job but once he'd tasted having his own business things would never be the same. He'd done his share of horse trading in the past and was ready to strike out on his own. Running the tool route with *Snap On* gave him a taste of being his own boss. But as an independent contractor, he was still reporting to someone else and it's no exaggeration to say he had a problem with authority. So he quit the route to do his own thing. Unfortunately, he had absolutely no idea what that thing would be. In the meantime my mother picked up the slack financially, a true testament to the strong woman she had become.

I mentioned in the introduction that at one point my mom ran a daycare center out of our home. The extra income dad earned on the tool route enabled them to build a separate room for the operation onto the side of our house. Named simply "The Addition", my father and uncles did most of the work themselves except for the plumbing and electrical work that was beyond their level of expertise. Equipped with a large play room, kitchenette, bathroom, and office for the paperwork, they were ready for business. Most of the clients came through word of mouth and the giant "Country Bumpkins Daycare" sign planted securely in our front yard. Soon mom had enough kids enrolled to justify hiring a full time staff. And although getting some of the parents to pay was like pulling teeth, the daycare was profitable from the beginning.

This extra income helped lessen the blow when my father quit the tool industry. Not long after, he learned of a small ice cream parlor for sale and became very excited at the prospect of owning his own business. After coming back from Vietnam, he had a great deal of trouble taking orders from other people. With the restaurant coming available, this looked like the opportunity he'd been waiting for. The owners were very motivated to sell which worked out well for my dad because he was more than ready to buy. Once the details got worked out, including using our house as collateral, my father owned his very first café. He couldn't have been more proud.

Both parents were spending tremendous amounts of time and energy trying to ensure the success of their respective business endeavors. And their efforts were paying great dividends even though most small businesses fail in the first five years. Witnessing how much sweat equity they invested makes me prone to think the primary reason for those failures is simply a matter of exhaustion. It's incredibly difficult to run things by yourself and equally hard finding suitable employees to help bear the load. Not only was mom charged with the task of watching the children, when the daycare shut down for the evening her night was far from over. There was still plenty of paperwork and cleanup left undone at the end of the day. My father's situation wasn't much different as the two of them spent countless nights burning the candle at both ends. Eventually, my mother grew weary from carrying such a stressful workload and decided to close down "Country Bumpkins" forever. She'd been running it for long enough. The kids that started at the daycare as infants were nearly ready to enter kindergarten when she chose to call it quits. If only my dad could've been so lucky.

The restaurant was located in a strip mall just outside of town. The center was anchored by two large chain stores, *Winn Dixie* (grocery store) and *TG&Y* (small discount retailer), and most of his business spilled over from their existing traffic. It wasn't long before a *Wal-Mart* was built closer to town devastating the smaller discounter's bottom line. They just couldn't keep up with the retailing behemoth and shut their doors shortly thereafter. It took a hit, but the small outdoor mall still had adequate traffic shopping at the grocery store that still remained. Things took a turn for the worse however when dad got news of their plans to relocate. With the new shopping center being built so much closer to civilization, people weren't willing to drive a few extra miles just to get groceries, much less to buy an ice cream cone. As he watched them lock the doors of *Winn Dixie* the final time he knew that the restaurant, and our family's entire future, was in serious trouble.

6

"Fish out of Water"

Losing the two biggest retailers in the strip center made it impossible for the restaurant to survive. There simply wasn't enough traffic to keep it afloat. He tried everything he could think of to keep the doors open. Some of his more loyal customers who lived nearby continued their patronage, but it was too little too late. Pretty soon the store wasn't even generating enough cash flow to pay the utilities, much less the rent on the building. He tried to terminate the lease early thinking he could move to a busier part of town, but the landlord wouldn't budge. The restaurant was responsible for the full term of the contract, not to mention all the money still owed for all the financed equipment. He sold what he could to another entrepreneur but never received a single payment. The bank didn't care why he couldn't pay they just wanted their money. So, with everything tied to the one asset my parents had left to their name, they came after our house next.

Entering the final phase of foreclosure, our time in Lake City was rapidly coming to an end. The last thing in the world I wanted was to be uprooted from all my friends in the middle of the school year. We'd lived there so long I never thought we'd leave. At least not until after I graduated high school. I'm sure it's not exactly what my parents had in mind either. But a lack of job options for my father left them no other choice.

My mom's younger sister Cherie and her husband had moved to Atlanta a few years prior opening a restaurant of their own. Thriving in the growing metropolitan market they were considering the idea of expanding into delivery. With dad's years of food experience he was perfect to head up this new arm of their business. So he swallowed his pride and we prepared for the move. It all happened so fast I barely had time to say goodbye to my friends. They could hardly believe we were leaving so soon. We didn't talk about it much those final two weeks. I guess some things in life are better left unspoken.

My father and brother moved first as my mom worked out the final days at her job. They moved in temporarily with her older sister, Marcia, and waited for our arrival. Dad was already working at the restaurant when we got there. We were going to stay with Marcia until my mother found a new job. She was gracious enough to allow us the use of her dining room, turning it into a bedroom until we could get ourselves situated. It was difficult cramming so many people into that house but we managed to survive. Despite our many differences, the family always seems to be there when you need them.

At this point, dad was making decent money on his delivery route and mom seemed anxious to start a new career. I think she could sense the growing tension in my aunt's house and wanted to reclaim a home of her own. She'd always enjoyed her days of banking so she figured that was as good a place as any to start. Armed with a strong background in the industry, and persistent distribution of her resume to key contacts, she was able to land a decent job in no time. A small bank took immediate interest and, recognizing her outstanding leadership skills, promoted her to an officer's position soon thereafter.

The new job provided my mother with a newfound sense of security. Her career in banking looked very promising and she was ready to move into her own home. It wouldn't be easy to buy another house with the recent foreclosure back in Florida. But one thing about my mom, she's incredibly persistent when she wants something bad enough. And she wanted a house.

The first step of her plan was renting a small three bedroom place located a stones throw from my new high school. It was right across the street from a great park, providing all the comforts of home young boys need. There were baseball fields, tennis courts, and a full size gym where we could play basketball. For an avid sports lover like me, having such easy access to the facilities was incredibly convenient. Mom was always up for a game of tennis.

Ok, time for a brief timeout. I hope you don't mind too much. I'll return to the story in just a moment. Writing the last sentence of the previous paragraph seems to have jarred loose horrible memories of torture from my youth. And to think my very own mother was to blame. Thinking about playing tennis reminded me of the time she signed me up for lessons. She wanted to broaden my horizons by exposing me to other activities besides baseball. Back then, I lived and breathed for the sport. Sure we'd play the occasional backyard, no pads, tackle football game, but only once in a while. Mostly it was baseball, baseball, and more baseball. That's all I was interested in, especially after diving for the football resulted in a broken pinky finger and yet another trip to the local emergency room. Thank goodness they had my room ready. Other sports were just never quite as appealing to me as baseball. But my mom had good intentions so I guess I can't blame her for trying to open my eyes to another sport or two. My problem was with her choices.

Stepping onto the tennis court for my first lesson, I quickly realized that there wasn't another boy anywhere in sight. Not one. There were young pre-teen girls covering every inch of the court, and I was rapidly approaching estrogen overload. Had this happened two or three years later I'd have been in heaven. But as a young boy of only nine years old, I wasn't yet interested in the opposite sex. So instead of being in heaven, it was more like a living hell as I ran screaming off the court, chasing my mother down at the car and demanding she take me home immediately. That was the extent of my illustrious career in tennis. Mom was disappointed that I was unwilling to play, but would have her revenge soon enough.

The next "sport" she selected for me to try was worse than a horrible nightmare. I literally cried out in terror when she announced she'd signed me up for gymnastics. Now I realize there are many athletic, highly talented, male gymnasts out there who are experts in their field. And I'm sure that many years of hard work have gone into perfecting their craft. But to me, it wasn't exactly the kind of sport I had in mind. At least she enrolled Kevin in the class with me so I didn't have to take the embarrassment alone. Misery loves company. Don't get me wrong, I wasn't exactly a willing participant. I did go, but not without begging my mother repeatedly to let us quit first. This time though, she wouldn't cave and forced us against our will to attend the lessons. It was the worst kind of torture imaginable.

Again grouped together with all girls, we reluctantly went through the motions until it was finally over. Those one hour classes were some of the longest, most agonizing moments of my life. My mom never did understand what all the fuss was about. She didn't think it was any big deal. What on earth was I thinking? We were learning such valuable skills (like how to do a proper round-off) that were sure to come in handy later on in life. Come on, I'm a guy. I shouldn't even know what a round-off is, much less how to do one. All I can say is thanks, mom, for the deep emotional scars your experimenting has caused me. Thanks a lot.

Now where was I? Oh yes, the park across the street from our house. Sporting facilities weren't the only thing Wills Park had to offer. We spent many hours in the wilderness building forts and playing war. By this point, John and Matt were living with us and they, along with Kevin, absolutely loved exploring the great outdoors. Kevin used an old wooden ammo box my dad picked up at a garage sale to haul around their equipment. He kept the coolest stuff in there, ranging from throwing knives to a healthy supply of M-80's, just in case he ever had to blow something up. At the time, ninja movies were also extremely popular and he had more than his share of Chinese stars.

But my favorite item was the *Rambo* inspired survival knife Kevin purchased at the local flea market. Those things were awesome. The blade was about five inches long and plenty sharp for our purposes. Across the back were a series of ridges designed to either scale a fish, or saw a branch, whatever the situation called for. The handle was a four inch long, hollow cylinder capped off by a round compass. Unscrewing the cap revealed a number of useful items stored securely inside the hollow handle. Needles, waterproof matches, fishing line, and more were right at our fingertips should we ever need them. If it was good enough for *Rambo*, then it was good enough for us. Yes sir, Kevin kept all of his most prized possessions inside that box, at least until mom found his dirty magazine collection hidden inside. It was *her* ammo box after that.

Dad saw nothing wrong with it saying, "He has to learn sometime." But mom disagreed, feeling it was inappropriate for a twelve year old boy, or any age for that matter, to be exposed to such graphic material. I think she was right. She stood her ground with my father and not only did Kevin lose the use of his ammo box, he spent the next two weeks grounded for his misbehavior.

When you're on a limited income, you have to be creative when it comes to entertainment. Things like navigating creeks in search of crawdads, though incredibly fun, can become somewhat mundane after awhile. That's when mom came to the rescue. She suggested we play a variation of hide and go seek in our own backyard. It would begin at night since the limited visibility made the game much more challenging. We'd pick sides and one team would be given two minutes to run outside and find a hiding spot. Mom was not only the inventor of "Sneak Around in the Dark" but an active participant as well. She has a strong mischievous side to her that no one believes when I tell them. But it's true. And it was her outrageous actions that helped the game evolve into the legacy it is today.

Playing opposite her team one clear summer night, I darted outside as they started the timer and found a perfect place to hide. Like the days playing board games with John, I soon found myself playing a game within a game. While they were getting ready to sprint outside looking for us I wasn't very concerned about being found. My objective was simply to determine just how much I could scare somebody. So I hid on the corner of the house waiting for someone to come running around it. And that someone happened to be my mom. Unfortunately for me however, was her decision to create a game of her own as well. She thought it would be hilarious to carry a big plastic cup full of water outside with her to prove when she'd found someone. And boy did she ever find someone. As she rounded the corner, I jumped directly in her path and yelled "Boo!" getting completely soaked in the process. Complaining that her tactics were unfair, she was quick to point out that it was my fault for trying to scare her in the first place. From that point forward a new game was born and "Water Wars" was here to stay.

Lots of experience playing hide-and-go-seek helped me become especially talented at discovering inconspicuous hiding spots. My small frame enabled me to fit where the other kids couldn't, or wouldn't, go. Kitchen cabinets, washing machines and dryers turned out to be fantastic hideaways. The best part was that I could use them over and over again since people rarely found me. They often gave up quickly, going to the designated location to cover their eyes and wait for my return. This allowed me to get back in the game without ever compromising my position. My unusual hiding spots did cause a bit of a problem once though when my mom nearly turned the dryer on with me still tucked away quietly inside.

Of all the times we played "Water Wars", the highlight for me was getting the best of my cousin John yet again. As if he hadn't already gotten enough abuse from me in his lifetime. It was that smart mouth of his that kept causing a problem. We always seem to dislike the same traits in others that we dislike about ourselves. At any rate, as far as I was concerned he deserved whatever he got. And he got it good that night. Combining my talent for climbing with a natural ability to finding hiding places, I was able to take the game to a whole new level. In the back of our house, just outside the sliding glass door, sat a patio enclosed on all sides by a tall wooden fence. This wasn't the first time I'd used the fence to climb on top of the house. However, it was the first time I devised a method for dragging a full bucket full of water up there with me. It took a heck of a lot of planning to pull the whole thing off in the two minutes we were allotted to hide. But the payoff was definitely worth it. I waited patiently above the door until John finally took the bait. The moment he stepped outside, gallons of water came crashing down on top of him. He was completely drenched. I don't know if he was angrier about being so wet or because of how hard I was laughing at his expense. If I wasn't careful I'd have fallen clean off the roof.

For as many fights I had with John, there was still a silent war raging between Kevin and I as our sibling rivalry continued to cause us problems. We were fighting like cats and dogs one night when my mom broke down crying. It was strange to see her react in that way, it usually took a great deal of effort to break her down. But it wasn't just our constant fighting that was bothering her. The news she had for us would change our world forever. She called us both into the living room and said, "There's no easy way for me to tell you this so I'll just come right out and say it, I'm pregnant." What a total shock. She was 36 years old and believed her child rearing days were over. Apparently, God had other ideas. She was very emotional at the idea of bringing another child into the world. With her career in full swing, the thought of the added responsibility a newborn brings made her weak in the knees. But somehow, she managed to survive.

My war with Kevin took a temporary hiatus as we did everything in our power to help mom during her pregnancy. And nine months later we had a new kid brother, Jeffrey, in the family. Kevin was already twelve when Jeff was born, much too large an age gap for him to enjoy the bullying privileges I'd gotten with him. His only alternative was to continue the ongoing battle with me. And to make sure he knew we were still at odds, I sent him a message one afternoon he couldn't ignore.

Mom often bought multiple bottles of baby powder when she found them on sale, storing the extras underneath her bathroom sink. If memory serves, I was searching for more cotton swabs to replenish the supply in our bathroom. But I became sidetracked by the sight of all that baby powder and a most devious thought ran through my mind. Grabbing one of the bottles I headed straight for the living room where Kevin was quietly watching after school cartoons. Mom was still at work and we had the whole house to ourselves that day. The war we'd been fighting was still on hold but that was getting ready to change in a hurry. I walked into the room and stood between Kevin and the television set as a wicked smirk ran across my mouth. Removing an economy size bottle of baby powder from behind my back, I aimed it at Kevin and squeezed it with all my might. That's when the top went flying off covering every inch of his body with the fine white dust. He was furious. The next thing I knew he'd ran to my mom's bathroom to retrieve some ammunition of his own. I was laughing so hard I barely noticed he was missing. He returned with two bottles, one for each hand, to exact his revenge. The ensuing action wasn't pretty and by the time we were finished not a single container of baby powder remained unopened anywhere in the house.

When mom got home and saw the mess we made in her living room she didn't say a word. She just dropped to her knees and started to cry. The stress of raising a family while working a full time job was beginning to take its toll. There was simply nothing left at the end of the day to deal with us boys. We didn't help matters much with our constant bickering and roughhousing. Seeing her kneeling on the floor at her wit's end must've sank in because we finally put an end to our lifelong feud.

Speaking of feuds, you may find it interesting to know that we are real life descendents from one of the families that started it all. Almost everyone is familiar with the infamous story about the Hatfield's and McCoy's. Living in the hills of West Virginia (of course), these two families literally hated each other for years. The dispute apparently originated over a love affair gone bad. Kind of like a redneck version of *Romeo and Juliet*. It was hardly a shock to find out we were related to such an unruly bunch. At least we can be certain of our southern heritage, tracing it back to so many fully certifiable rednecks. As if there were ever any doubt.

With most of the fighting coming to an abrupt end, I needed something else to occupy my time. Luckily, baseball was coming around soon and tryouts for the fourteen year old league were to be held across the street at the park. After trying out we got a call from the coach two days later letting me know I would be playing on the Atlanta Braves. How great was that? Getting to play for the hometown favorite was a huge thrill for me. The teams in Lake City were all locally sponsored bearing names like Rossi Hardware, Barnett Bank, and more. But these were named after professional baseball teams from the major leagues.

Putting on that jersey for the first time I felt a strong sense of pride and accomplishment. It's just too bad that feeling didn't translate itself onto the diamond. As a team, we were horrible. Individually, there was a great deal of talent amongst the group but we couldn't seem to pull it together on the field. No matter how hard we tried the end result was always the same. During the regular season we lost every single game we played. It was awful. Not to mention extremely embarrassing. Kids on the other team looked forward to matching up against us, figuring it would result in an easy win. And they were right. We were the biggest laughing stock of the entire league. I'm sure every guy on the team wanted to give up at some point, but we weren't a bunch of quitters. If we were going to keep on losing, we were going to do it together.

Not everyone on the team felt the same sense of unity as the rest of the group. One kid decided his best course of action was to take the easy way out, hanging up his cleats after a few early losses. He was incredibly arrogant about his ability and walked out on us. As he was leaving he said he refused to play baseball with a bunch of losers. What a pathetic excuse for a teammate. The funny thing is, he wasn't even very talented. Nobody really cared that he was leaving. Heck, with him gone we'd probably have a better shot at winning a game or two. But I must admit, the comments he made about the team stung a little. It also bothered some of the guys that he got in the last word. Or did he?

The rest of the season was a total bust. That is until it came time for the play-offs. Playing back in Florida I never experienced anything like this. The idea of extra games tacked onto the end of the schedule was a foreign concept to me. But if it meant getting to play more baseball I was all for it. Besides, the slate from the regular season was wiped clean and each team was placed in a double elimination tournament for the league championship. After the year we had, we had absolutely no reason to be optimistic about our chances of winning the title. But that's exactly how we felt. An air of confidence came over the team and a funny thing began to happen. We started winning. Most of the teams still grossly underestimated us and the wins kept coming. The feeling was indescribable as we came back from a horrible showing in the regular season all the way to the finals, ultimately reaching the championship game. This was for all the marbles. The contest was very close and it came right down to the wire. I'll never forget watching our first baseman step on the bag for the final out. It was incredible. Needless to say, our parents could not have been prouder of our accomplishment. They understood what a tremendous victory this was, not only for the team, but to each of us as individuals.

The coaches and parents got together arranging for us to take a group trip to *Six Flags over Georgia* as a reward for our effort. What a great idea. We loaded up the minivans and SUV's and headed off to a fun filled day at the amusement park. There were so many of us that we broke up into groups shortly after getting inside. It would be much easier for three or four of us to hang out than for all fifteen to try and navigate the park together. Most of the rides only sat four people at a time anyway, so it worked out better in smaller groups.

All of a sudden one of the guys spotted the kid who quit our team walking around the park with a couple of his friends. We were having so much fun riding the roller coasters that we almost didn't notice him. Thank goodness we didn't let that opportunity get away. Not holding a grudge, we stopped to talk with him for a minute. Recognizing us as former teammates, he asked what brought us to the park that day. It was pure poetic justice getting to tell him how the season ultimately turned out. And to top it off, we knew he'd be running into other guys from the team all day long.

I'm glad it was so memorable because that turned out to be the last year I'd ever play organized baseball. During my first year of high school I learned that tryouts for the freshman baseball team were coming soon. When they finally arrived though, I'd come down with a horrible case of the flu and my mother urged me to sit out and wait for next year. But I tried out anyway hoping to tough it out and make the team. That's not quite how things turned out. I didn't even make it past the first cut. And there was no one to blame except myself. Weakened from the sickness, I could barely hit the ball out of the infield during batting practice. And forget about getting to those sharply hit ground balls at second base. From the coaches perspective it must've looked like I had no business even showing up in the first place. The experience was very demoralizing and I drifted away from the game after a full year off from playing. Baseball had always been such a passion of mine. It was a shame to throw it all away over one bad outing. But that's exactly what I did, and I've regretted it ever since.

High school was a very challenging time in my life. Leaving my hometown was still affecting me and I was in no hurry to make close friendships only to have them taken away again. As a result, I was extremely introverted and didn't attend a dance or football game in all four years. Not a single one. It was no fun feeling like such an outsider, isolated from any kind of social interaction with my peers. I couldn't seem to make friends as easily as I did back in Lake City. All I wanted to do was go back home. The idea dominated my thoughts. But it just wasn't going to happen.

Things continued like this until the end of my senior year. That's when I started hanging out with a couple guys named Chris and Jason. I already knew Chris from that magical year playing with him on the Braves. During the last quarter before graduation, we also had the last two classes of the day together. Before that we were only acquaintances. But there's just something about sitting around in a Sociology class, after sweating profusely in P.E. the period before that tends to bond people. One day he asked me if I wanted to go bowling that Friday night with him, Jason, and their good friend Jay. It sounded like fun so I agreed to go. And it was fun. In fact, we had such a good time that we spent nearly every other day that summer hanging out. Most of those nights were spent at the local bowling alley. If we didn't want to bowl, there was always the option of playing pool. Or we could head back over to Jay's apartment and play cards or video games. It felt great to have good friends back in my life again.

7

"A Higher Education"

According to most of the popular stereotypes, rednecks don't have much in the way of formal education. In fact, many people believe they usually don't even make it past grade school. Well that's where I'm different. I passed every single class I took until reaching high school, and only failed one there. Heck, I know you might find this hard to imagine, but this is one redneck that even attended college. Now before you get the wrong idea, I should tell you that I dropped out of school before graduating. Quite a shame too since I would've been the first person in my family to have earned such an honor.

So, what was the problem? Why did I put in such a hard time at school for nearly three years before deciding to take a different path in life? It wasn't that I couldn't handle the university curriculum. I had very little trouble passing courses many of the other students were struggling to get through. Some of them even wanted me to join their study group after scoring a perfect 100 on the first Physics test of the semester. Therein lies the problem, how could I join their study group when I never studied? But I'm getting a little ahead of myself. To get the full scope of my illustrious career at Georgia Southern University we must go all the way back to my senior year of high school.

With graduation day approaching rapidly, it began to dawn on me just how little attention I had given to my future. The rest of the student body was busy talking with counselors, eagerly sending off applications to the colleges of their choice. Here I was cruising along as if divine intervention was going to pave the way for me. While there's no doubt in my mind that a higher power has had a tremendous impact on my life, I cannot underestimate the effect of free will. That is to say that although the path may have been laid out before me, I still had to choose which way to go when faced with a fork in the road. Unfortunately, the time left to make that choice was dwindling fast as high school graduation was right around the corner.

After sharing the situation with Chris, he suggested I go to Georgia Southern with him and Jason. They already had an apartment lined up and assured me it would be no problem to stay with them. Jason would share his room with me, lightening the financial burden on both of them since the rent would now be split three ways instead of two. All I needed to do now was submit an application to the school and talk it over with the folks.

The first part was easy. Throughout high school my grades in the areas of math and science were very good. Both subjects came naturally to me, so when my counselor recommended pursuing the field of engineering, it seemed like the logical direction to go. She really wanted me to apply to Georgia Tech first, saying that even though my GPA was only slightly above average, my math SAT score might be enough to get me in the door. But I had other ideas in mind. After such an introverted high school career, I was in no hurry to spend my college years doing nothing but cracking the books. And that's exactly what I had to look forward to if I'd chosen to go to Georgia Tech. So I made the wise decision to pick a school based on nothing other than the simple fact my two best friends were going there. Actually, Georgia Southern had a special program for certain engineering students designed to get them ready to transfer to Tech. Chris was already signed up for the program and I knew if there was any chance of convincing my parents to let me go, this was it.

For those of you who may not be aware, Georgia Southern isn't especially well known for its academic curriculum. In fact, if you were to poll all the high school students in the state you'd likely find that over 90% of them know it primarily as a party school. Education is a secondary concern for most newly enrolling freshman. The ironic thing is that it's actually a fully accredited University, meaning the curriculum there is just as rigorous and demanding as any other school in the state. The main difference is that the entry standards are substantially lower and the drop out rate is much higher. They'll let almost anybody in, or at least they used to, but graduating is an entirely different story. Combine lower entering SAT scores and high school GPA's with the ease of getting alcohol under age (one gas station near campus was named *Fast N Easy*), and you've got a recipe for disaster. Of the twelve or so people that I'm still in contact with who attended school there, only one has an actual diploma with the words "Georgia Southern University" inscribed across the top. So you can imagine the challenge I had before me trying to convince my mother to let me attend school down there with two of my best friends.

Chris and Jason had already made the arrangements for a two bedroom apartment conveniently located a short bike ride from campus. We'd become much better friends over the summer and they insisted I should go to school down there too. It didn't take much to convince me. My agenda for choosing this particular school had nothing to do with academia. There was no real thought of how good the education would be, nor what kind of career opportunities it would provide. Spending high school locked inside an emotional cage of low self esteem, I was excited at the prospect of breaking out in college. Besides, I'd finally been able to make some good friends and I wasn't anxious to see them leave without me. So I set out to try and convince my parents of the benefits of attending college such a long way from home, in the small town of Statesboro, Georgia.

Fortunately, neither my mother nor my father had any previous knowledge of the school's reputation. If they'd discovered what I'd heard about it, I wouldn't have had a snowball's chance in hell of ever going to school down there. As it was, it still took weeks of consistent effort before I was able to wear them down. Mom was mostly concerned about my being so far away from home. Getting a car of my own and promising to come home on the weekends helped put her mind at ease. Dad was easier and even seemed kind of excited about me stepping out on my own. It turned out that the school had an excellent engineering program specifically geared toward preparing students for transfer to Georgia Tech. With my high school grades and SAT math scores, I was able to be accepted for this program. It was enough to seal the deal with the folks and I was on my way.

Arriving on campus was a quite a shock. I still couldn't believe we were going to have our own apartment at a major university. It was just too good to be true. But that's precisely what the future held in store for us. The wheels of change had already been set in motion and it was only a matter of time before I was a college man. Drawing the smallest straw, Jason won the task of driving the big U-Haul truck down to Statesboro. It was only a three and a half hour drive from our Atlanta suburb to the university campus. But for an eighteen year old young man, the idea of cruising down the interstate in a twenty four foot moving truck was slightly intimidating. Chris and I provided encouragement and the necessary emotional support to get the show on the road. He ended up doing a remarkable job of driving, managing to arrive with all our stuff, and himself, fully intact.

We finished unpacking and enjoyed the week off we had before classes began. It gave us a chance to decorate our new pad, giving the place a personal touch making it feel more like home. Jason, who'd worked at Blockbuster Video while still in high school, had accumulated an enormous collection of movie posters for our new apartment. We went to work with a step ladder and staplers covering every inch of the living room wall in just a couple hours. Once that was done, we still had plenty of posters left over and decided to cover the vault ceiling as well.

When we finished, our wall to wall movie poster motif looked spectacular. It was like someone had ripped a page right out of *Redneck Interior Design Quarterly*. I added my personal flair for style by stapling used Slim Jim wrappers on the wall next to the light switch. Now this was a college apartment worthy of bachelor pad status. All that was left was to fill it with young college women.

Unfortunately, girls would have to be put on the back burner temporarily as our upcoming class schedules took top priority. We'd already finished registration and were anxiously awaiting our first day of classes. The first two years involved mostly core curriculum designed to help us mature into well rounded adults. The work involved was less than I'd anticipated and I was glad to discover most of my professors didn't have an attendance policy. As long as the students could do the work, it didn't matter to them how often they showed up. This was perfect for me since I learned better by reading the book anyway.

There was one professor who wanted the best of both worlds. He listed in the course syllabus that there was no attendance policy required for his Calculus III course. His theory was that if students didn't show up, it would be impossible for them to pass the course. When Chris and I took his class things turned out much differently than he anticipated. As much as we enjoyed cutting classes, we both knew how critical the math and science courses were to our program of study. Without developing a solid foundation in both of them we could kiss a future in engineering goodbye. So, we attended class diligently when it came to those two subjects. Except the time we signed up for this guy's course.

Listening to him speak the first day it was clear how much of a prick he was. He had an air of superiority about him that turned us off immediately. Chris looked over at me and without speaking a word I knew that this was one math class we wouldn't be attending regularly. It was hard enough sticking around that first day. The guy just kept carrying on about how challenging the course would be and how important he was. He also made darn sure to tell us about the textbook he'd written that was being used at Georgia Tech. He was a legend in his own mind.

Other than the test days, we might've shown up for class a total of ten other times that semester. And the only reason we came that much was to find out if he'd changed the test dates. It wasn't like we hadn't given him a chance. After surviving that terrible first day, we discussed the issue and decided to give him the benefit of the doubt. But a week later our minds were left unchanged. Although the course syllabus clearly stated there would be no attendance policy, it was obvious he was growing increasingly frustrated with our absences. Furthermore, we were both passing the class preventing him from making an example out of us to the rest of the class.

I think it was eating him up that a couple of college guys were getting the best of him. Sitting in the computer lab one day I found out just how bothered he really was. We'd taken a test a few days prior and he handed back our exams as we worked on our projects. Looking down at my paper, I thought my score was unusually low considering how good I felt about the material. Sitting at my desk wondering how I was going to pass the course, one of the girls in the class broke my concentration. She was positively giddy with excitement as she bragged to her friends about the grade she'd received. Naturally I asked to see her paper to determine exactly where I'd gone wrong.

Using her test to check my own answers, something strange began to dawn on me. From the looks of things I should've scored higher than she did, not the other way around. After taking enough time to confirm my suspicions, I marched right up to his desk at the front of the lab and demanded an explanation. He stammered around a bit before finally attempting to explain the discrepancy by claiming my mistakes were fundamental errors. I knew exactly what he was trying to say. The only problem with his theory was that he was dead wrong, and he knew it. If anything, she was the one who didn't have a solid understanding of the material covered. But she was in attendance every day and frequently even spent time at his office. She was your typical teacher's pet. I thought for sure that kind of stuff only happened in high school.

By now the discussion had turned into a full blown argument that he ended by saying, "Well it's just too bad you didn't come to class more often, you might have gotten a better grade." That last remark infuriated me and I responded by shouting, "What's too bad is that you can't teach because if you could I'd have been in class!" I followed it up by flinging my backpack through the open doorway and stormed out into the hallway. Chris came running out after me saying, "Man, you just told that professor off good. That was awesome!" Even though I'd let my temper get the better of me, it felt good to stand up for what's right.

Fortunately the semester was almost over and the only test we had left was the final exam. I studied diligently but didn't expect a snowball's chance in hell of getting a passing grade. Not after the stunt I pulled in front of all the other students. Test day came and I refused to even make eye contact with the man as I handed in my paper. He never admitted any wrongdoing but he didn't have to. We were both keenly aware of the injustice that had taken place that day. About a week later he spotted me checking the grade postings and actually tried to make amends. I guess he realized his error in judgment because he told me I'd done very well on the test and was getting a B in the class. Then he asked if that was alright with me. If he'd graded me based on my own merit the best I could've hoped for was as C. Needless to say I was more than satisfied with my final grade.

I'm glad to have missed so many of that professor's classes. It wasn't like I missed anything worthwhile. The time that would've been spent listening to another boring lecture was put to good use honing my skills with the ladies. And believe me, they definitely needed some work.

By now I was getting pretty tired of being left out from having any kind of social life. Four years of high school was enough, it was time for me to finally come out of my shell. As the alcohol flowed so did my confidence and my luck with the ladies improved dramatically. Bryan affectionately referred to this phenomenon as having "liquid personality". Unfortunately for him, most nights he had so much "personality" that he was passed out cold by ten o'clock. But I discovered that the moderate consumption of alcohol eased my nerves enough to leave a favorable impression on the females. It was purely a confidence issue. Having a drink or two gave me enough confidence to approach a girl I was interested in meeting. As a result, I began to drink socially while hanging out at parties. Slowly but surely I was finally beginning to come out of my shell.

Georgia Southern is known primarily for only two things, great parties and good looking women. And they usually went hand in hand. The bar scene was pretty popular down there but nothing came close to the keg parties. And of all the keggers I've been to my good friend Billy threw the best ones. Known as Hillbilly to his friends, this guy organized some of the greatest parties ever put together in the history of the school. His motivation was simple. He wanted to get drunk and he didn't want to pay for it. So he started thinking, ultimately creating what amounted to a full blown business plan for accomplishing his objective.

At any party, the standard cost for drinking off the keg was three dollars per person. He did a little quick math and realized that at that rate, it wouldn't take much to turn a profit, if he could get enough students to show up. So he used a little southern ingenuity to draw the people in.

First he made the parties a regular Friday night event. Since most of the student body went home on the weekends, everyone left in town would have something entertaining to do. Pretty soon his shin-digs gained so much notoriety around campus that people actually started staying in town just to attend. But they would never have grown in popularity so quickly if not for his next idea.

When he ran his thoughts by the guys, they thought he was absolutely crazy. But not me, I felt his ideas were ingenious and couldn't wait to help put them in motion. We happened to be friends with some freshman girls and it was with their help that things began to take off. Taking a big risk, Billy told them of his proposition. Any girls at the party could drink off the keg all night for only a buck. This was hardly a good way to turn a profit, and if everyone got away so cheap he'd have lost money every time. However, if there's one rule about college life it's this. Wherever there's a bunch of freshman girls, you can bet the guys will find them. And that's exactly what happened. He lived in an upstairs apartment and the people spilled down the steps and out into the parking lot. Billy made a killing those nights sometimes raking in as much as $200 cash for his efforts. Not bad work for a budding entrepreneur. If only he'd applied more of those skills in the classroom.

Mixing alcohol with young college guys can sometimes lead to a rise in physical aggression. Fighting a lot himself (mostly losing), Billy decided to give a group of football players free beer if they'd keep an eye out for trouble. It worked like a charm. Those guys were huge and nobody wanted to mess with them. And just in case the cops showed up we had a remedy for that as well. My next door neighbor Tom was a few years older than us and had grown up in Statesboro. Because of that, he went to high school with most of the guys on the force and when one of them showed up he went out and smoothed things over. It was a beautiful setup.

Mind you, I'm not condoning any of the wild behavior or craziness that happened down at school. But you didn't really think you'd get through an entire book about rednecks without finding something in here about getting drunk did you? I'm sure you could've seen that one coming. Hitting the bottle is practically a birthright where I come from. That's why I fit in so well at Georgia Southern.

The reality is that most of the students were just seeking a sense of independence and just picked a poor way to spread their wings. I'm as guilty as anyone else when it came to drinking. Chalk it up to a lack of experience. Or maybe I just wanted to fit in with my group of friends. Whatever the case, you can't go back and change history. All you can do is learn from the past and make better choices in the future.

As crazy as we were at school, it doesn't even come close to a party a friend told me about. The rugby players at Georgia Southern were literally insane. Living directly across the street from their practice field, I'd watched them play on occasion and they were brutal. If you've never had the chance to watch this sport live, you'd be amazed at how crazy they are. Rarely do they wear any kind of protective equipment and yet still hit each other at full speed. It's sort of like watching full grown men play tackle football without wearing any pads. The guys who play are incredibly intense. I've never seen that kind of aggression acted out on a playing field before. Regular football doesn't even compare, these guys are out for blood. And they party just as hard as they play.

Although I only attended one rugby party down there it was more than enough. To this day it still ranks as the wildest, most out of control event I've ever witnessed. Held after every game they played, it was tradition to invite the other team over to party with them. Because of the rough nature of the sport, the guys that participate seem to have a common bond regardless of which team they play for. That certainly wasn't the case at this party. Sure they invited the other team back for the festivities. But once things got rolling, the guys from the other team left the party. I remember hearing one of them say, "We're out of here man, you guys are crazy!" That's quite a statement coming from a fellow rugby enthusiast.

At first things seemed normal enough. People were hanging around out back near the giant bonfire in the yard. Everyone was having a great time when all of a sudden, four players came running through the house carrying another guy on their shoulders while chanting rugby fight songs. He was lying face down, completely nude, with a piece of cardboard stuffed down between his two butt cheeks with the top of it lit on fire. They ran him proudly throughout the house before making a brief detour outside for the other guests to see. It was quite a spectacle. Then they took off back inside leaving the crowd wondering what in the hell was going on. This was the most bizarre thing I'd ever witnessed.

We later discovered that it was part of an elaborate ritual that every player on the team took part in when they scored their first goal. What an amazing honor. And it wasn't over yet. The guys reemerged this time on the rooftop, and proceeded to jump bare-assed onto the bonfire below. Apparently, they were drenched from head to toe as they'd hosed themselves off first as a precautionary measure. Yeah, like now this stunt was safe. What a bunch of lunatics. When they hit the ground, each one of them ran around the fire three times before joining hands and shouting their loyalty to each other in unison.

Once the craziness subsided, the party resumed and I guess standing naked in the middle of a fire can make you pretty thirsty because the beer didn't last much longer. So, after polishing off the first keg, they ran up to the *Fast N Easy* to grab another one. They went inside to pay after loading it on the truck and when they returned, the keg was gone. Someone had lifted it right off the back of their truck. With their reputation, no one expected something like this could happen. But it did happen and there was nothing they could do about it. The beer was gone and it wasn't coming back. So they bought another keg and went back to the party. They were extremely pissed off about the incident but weren't going to let it ruin their night.

Come to find out, one guy at the house had just left another party and overheard some guys from the swim team bragging about stealing a keg from the *Fast N Easy*. That was it, three of the guys hopped back in the truck and peeled out of the neighborhood. It took a total of a minute and a half for those three guys to walk inside, knock five guys out cold, and return to the vehicle keg in tow. They even got a bonus tap worth an extra $75 deposit for their trouble. Those poor swim team guys never even knew what hit them.

Don't get the wrong idea. There was more to college than going to parties. We did our share of partying but most of our days were spent just hanging out with friends. It was during our freshman year that we met one guy who left such an impression on us that he became unforgettable. Nothing would compare to the experience of knowing Dave.

The second year of school, we decided to find a new apartment and bring on another roommate to share the expenses. Locating a great townhouse for rent, Chris, Jason, and I asked Dave if he wanted to move in with us. Anxious to leave the dorm scene he readily agreed. And it wasn't long after living with Dave that we realized just how special he was.

It's not that Dave was stupid. In fact, it was quite the contrary. He did very well academically and had even applied to a renowned Art and Design school in neighboring Savannah. His artwork was truly phenomenal and we proudly displayed two of his earlier high school works on our living room wall. It was in the area of common sense that Dave fell a little short. In some ways he was incredibly naïve and we were all too happy to take advantage of him. For the longest time he believed I was colorblind and deaf in one ear from a fireworks accident. What a riot watching him speak into my good ear every time he thought I couldn't hear him. I was driving him and another buddy around town one afternoon when Dave leaned up from the backseat into the rearview mirror just so I could read his lips better. Now I admit to egging him a little but it didn't take much to keep him going.

Playing chess together one day he looked me dead in the face and asked how I was able to play if I was really colorblind. I responded by saying I memorized the location of the pieces at the beginning of the game and kept track of them until it was over. Taking it further, I went on to say that as the game went on it was harder to keep up and he had a better chance of winning the longer it took. He bought every word of it hook, line, and sinker. Occasionally I did feel bad about lying to him so much, but he was just such an easy target. There was even talk of telling him the truth but we felt it might overwhelm him potentially causing him to go into cardiac arrest. So we kept it going and I'm not sure if he knows the whole truth to this day. Of all the hell we gave Dave over the short time we'd known him, it was the one experience that didn't involve lying that left him scarred for the rest of his life.

We had all become very aware that increasing our muscularity would have an immediate impact on meeting girls. Not only would we be more attractive physically, but the increase in confidence would be worth its weight in gold. So we started using an off campus weight room to bulk up for the ladies. At first it seemed like an awful lot of effort and pain for little reward. But in time we began to see our muscles starting to swell.

On this particular day, Chris and I left the gym before Dave since he had a few more sets left to do before heading home. When we got home, we took turns flexing in the mirror at our pumped up biceps when Chris noticed a huge cockroach on the floor of the apartment. He is quite squeamish around bugs, especially spiders, so I quickly grabbed a shoe and moved toward the insect. To my surprise, Chris grabbed my arm saying "Wait, I have an idea." Curious, I listened as he described his master plan.

First he ran into the kitchen and grabbed a piece of duct tape a few inches long. I could tell by the look on his face that he was going to enjoy what would follow. Holding the edges of the tape with both hands, he slowly reached down toward that mutated bug with the sticky side down. "Got it!" he exclaimed as he gently lifted the bug off the ground, the tape firmly pressed against its back.

As soon as Dave entered the apartment I grabbed his attention pointing out that he looked like he got a great pump at the gym today. "Really," he said, "I didn't feel like I got much of a workout." "Oh yeah," I retorted, "those extra sets really look like they paid off. Why don't you check the mirror and see for yourself." Removing his shirt he began flexing his muscles, admiring the reflection he saw in the glass. "Maybe you're right...," was all he could utter before the unthinkable happened.

I must tell you that in my entire life I have never met anyone as scared of cockroaches as Dave was. He was absolutely petrified of them. When Chris slapped him across the back, sticking both sides of tape firmly to his bare skin, the look on his face was sheer terror. "What's was that?" he asked as he felt the legs of the roach tickling the middle of his back. Chris was already doubled over in laughter when he replied. "That my friend was the biggest damn cockroach I've ever seen anywhere!"

By this time Dave arms were flailing around wildly as he tried to remove the tape, but because his body was so tight from pumping iron he just couldn't seem to reach. All rational thought was gone as he went into a state of hysteria. Flinging the door open he darted outside screaming, "Get it off! Someone get this #@%!* thing off me!!"

I don't think I've ever laughed so hard in my entire life. The site of my roommate running around half naked in our parking lot, screaming at the top of his lungs, with a giant cockroach taped to his back was just too much for me to take.

Moving into the kitchen to regain my composure, I noticed a pack of sausages sitting out on the counter to defrost. My mom would jump at the chance to stock up on food whenever she found a good sale at the grocery store. Whatever she couldn't use right away would be frozen for a later date. She must've gotten one heck of a deal on these particular meats because when I went home for the weekend our freezer was crammed full of them. She insisted that I take some back to school with me. At the time, I thought she was just looking out for her firstborn son. Now I realize she probably just needed more space in the cooler for her next trip to the store. Either way, my roommates and I ended up eating more miniature sausages in a few short weeks than most people eat in a lifetime. This should help explain the package left thawing on the kitchen countertop.

It was at this point that a most devious thought occurred to me. For some reason I didn't think Dave had had enough. The poor guy was still outside running around in the parking lot, waving his arms like a mad man for everyone to see. That's about the time I decided it would be a good idea for Chris and I to use these partially frozen mini-meats to add to Dave's misery. And that is exactly what we did. We chased him around with those processed-projectiles, firing them in his direction every chance we could. This didn't last long however, as we were still laughing uncontrollably and Chris thought one of the neighbors might have called the cops. I wonder if "Assault with a deadly sausage" or "Intent to frighten with a live cockroach" would have gotten us much time.

Needless to say Dave never forgave us. Honestly, I don't blame him a bit for holding a grudge. We were way out of line acting in such manner with a complete disregard for his feelings. But that's exactly what we were, a couple of immature college kids getting our laughs at someone else's expense. And, more often than not Dave was the butt of our jokes. In the event he's reading this right now, I'd like to extend a heartfelt apology for the torture we put him through at school. My biggest regret is that he was so deathly afraid of cockroaches, if it weren't such a phobia he might've been able to tolerate our prank a little better. At any rate, it still ranks as one of the most hilarious things I have ever seen.

Yep, those days affectionately referred to as "the college experiment" will live in my memory forever. It was a wonderful time of self discovery. And although my transcripts remain incomplete, my time down there was not spent in vain. I learned that even rednecks have a shot at getting a college degree. The fountain of knowledge is meant for everyone, especially those whose cups are the emptiest. Heck, I'm proud to have gotten through two years of engineering classes. Those were three of the best years of my life. And little did I realize back then, but that school would also be the place I'd meet my future wife.

8

"Our Redneck Wedding"

During my third and final year of school at Georgia Southern, my friend Brooke had two of her girlfriends drive down to see her over the weekend. Although they both seemed like nice girls, at the time I didn't give it a second thought. Sure I flirted with them when they visited our apartment, but there was no way I could have ever predicted one of them would eventually become my wife.

Shannon loves to retell the story of meeting me for the first time. You see, I had just broken up with my girlfriend Julie and truth be told I was still somewhat bitter. So after downing a few beers and cursing out her answering machine, I was oblivious to the people hanging out at our place that afternoon. According to Shannon, she'd just sat down on the couch when I reached toward the dart board on the wall behind her, situated about a foot above her head. Offering no apology for climbing over this beautiful young woman I'd never even met, I fixed a wallet size picture of Julie in her cheerleading outfit right in the middle of the board. Then, I grabbed the five remaining darts (I used one to hold up the picture) and stepped back five steps from the edge of the couch.

"Hold still," I said calmly to Shannon as I began hurling darts at the picture sitting only inches above her head. Too scared to move, she covered her eyes until I'd finished throwing them all. When she finally stood up, she looked at me with amazement and said, "Are you crazy?!" At least that's how *she* claims it happened. All I can remember is hitting Julie directly in the face with all five darts. I was so impressed with my accomplishment that I passed the picture around the living room for everyone to admire. Shannon is convinced that hitting my target dead center while intoxicated, as well as her surviving the incident unscathed, was a sure sign we were meant to be together. Of course I'm sure that's not the first thought that came to mind about me as the darts whizzed overhead. But in time, she'd grow to love me.

After the weekend was over, she went back home and I never expected to see her again. But as luck would have it, I found myself back home sooner than expected after dropping out of school halfway through the semester. It was a lot to take in and the thought of having a girlfriend was the furthest thing from my mind.

I settled down from the breakup a few weeks later and began to feel sociable again. I remembered that Shannon and I seemed to get along rather well in the short time we'd spent together, so I asked Brooke if I could have her phone number. The first time I called she was out of town on Spring Break. Her father was very short on the phone and seemed less than pleased that I'd called. Nevertheless, he agreed to give her the message when she got back into town. It wasn't until three weeks later that my phone finally rang.

Apparently, her dad never relayed my message to her and when she found out that I'd called she was very excited. I felt like there was some chemistry between us that first weekend but you can never really be sure. What a relief to hear the reason she hadn't gotten in touch with me was all a big mistake. Normally I wouldn't have been so worked up over a girl I hardly knew. But for some reason there was a sense of nervous anxiety surrounding the idea of getting to see her again. So we talked over the phone a few times and agreed to go out on our first official date.

We agreed to meet near my house, settling on dinner and a movie for our evening out together. I don't usually like the idea of catching a flick on the first date because spending two hours in the theater makes it difficult to get to know each other. Unless of course the date's going badly, then getting a chance to escape by watching a movie can be the perfect way to enjoy two hours of silence. But that wasn't the case here. Shannon was great company during dinner. She had a wonderfully vibrant personality and we hit it off immediately, like two friends who'd known each other forever.

Things progressed slowly as we continued to date exclusively for over five years. That may seem like a long time, but we were both pretty young and in no real hurry to tie the knot. But neither of us wanted to see anybody else so we just kept dating with no pressure for anything more. Most of the girls I knew would've been pushing for a ring by then. Not Shannon. She was happy just being in the relationship with me. There was no reason to rush into anything, especially something as permanent as marriage.

My instincts were telling me this was the one but something was still holding me back. The truth is, I knew that somewhere deep down inside the idea was on her mind. But was I ready to make the ultimate commitment? And if I was able to get up the nerve to pop the question, would she say yes? Imagine if my assumptions were wrong and she turned me down cold. How humiliating would that be? What future could we possibly have after something like that? For the most part, I just kept pushing the idea out of my mind.

Shannon had the unique privilege of living in the state of Georgia her entire life. And by privilege, I mean death sentence. She was a purebred redneck through and through. Her hometown was a suburb of Atlanta, a little place called Stone Mountain, appropriately named for the big hunk of granite sitting in the middle of town. They even went so far as carving four Confederate heroes, including their horses, into the side of that giant rock. It's like having your own miniature redneck version of the famous Mount Rushmore.

She likes to refer to herself as a Southern Belle but that's really just a fancy name for a female redneck. How on earth could I go and fall for a redneck girl? Was listening to too much country music to blame? Did the lyrics of *"Give me a Redneck Girl"* somehow get etched into my brain, penetrating my subconscious and eliminating any chance of rational thought. If I did marry this girl, our future children wouldn't stand a chance. Every chromosome in their tiny little bodies would be infected with our mutated DNA. But I couldn't help my feelings and eventually asked Shannon to take my hand in marriage, sealing the fate of future generations in the same breath.

While we're on the subject of children, there's something we should go ahead and get out in the open. I am aware that a large segment of the population doesn't believe I should be legally allowed to procreate. They stand firm on their position, claiming that another generation of rednecks only serves to further contaminate society's gene pool. And that sounds great in theory, but they really don't have a leg to stand on. It's not like any of the normal folks are cross breeding with our kind. That'd be like mixing oil and water (it doesn't work). So who cares if we want to keep popping out youngsters one after another? Anyway, I guess we'll just have to cross that bridge when we get there.

Walking through the mall with Kevin one day it suddenly hit me. Shannon was the girl I wanted to spend the rest of my life with. There was no doubt in my mind that she was the one. But for some reason I didn't have the nerve to ask her to marry me. What in the world was I waiting on? Did I want her to get tired of waiting and break off the relationship? Of course not, I loved her deeply and the only thing standing in the way of us spending a lifetime together was me having the guts to ask. And it was that day in the mall that sealed the decision in my heart. We were in the middle of what was probably our biggest argument to date when everything became crystal clear. I realized nothing was ever going to change my love for her. So I gathered up every ounce of courage in my body and prepared to pop the question.

I proposed the day before Valentine's Day. Originally, my plan was to ask her on the actual holiday but I wasn't able to wait that long. After eating dinner at Red Lobster, we headed back to my mom's house to watch a movie. That's when it happened. Being so comfortable with Shannon, I never expected to be nervous about this day. But I was absolutely petrified. My legs trembled as the moment approached. Filled with anticipation, the rest of the family excused themselves from the room so we could be alone. I pulled the box from my jacket pocket and held it open in front of her. Shocked with disbelief she asked, "What is that?!" To which I replied, "What do you think it is?" Then she squealed with delight and hugged me tight. I was so nervous that the poor girl ended up having to remind me to get down on one knee to ask her properly. Damn, I knew I'd forgotten something. Fortunately she said yes anyway and the decision was made. We were getting married.

The yearlong engagement went by quickly. Setting the date for early March gave us plenty of time to prepare for the event. However, time flew by fast and before we knew it our wedding day was just around the corner. Thankfully, Shannon took the lead in the planning department. Looking back, I definitely could've been more helpful, but thanks to her things turned out great without much input from me. It wasn't that I didn't want to be involved. It's just that most of the specifics regarding the ceremony were more her department than they were mine. I didn't have much of a preference when it came to how many flowers we'd have or what kind of cake to get for the reception.

Instead, I turned my attention to the upcoming bachelor party my friends were getting ready for. Most men get to experience a blowout bash, a rite of passage if you will, before they slap on the handcuffs of love. And I'm sure that getting to send their buddy off into the great unknown with one final hurrah meant a lot to each of them. Oh, who am I kidding? It's just another excuse to party. At least that's how it was with my friends. They'd use anything under the sun as a reason to tie one on. But this, this was a special occasion. Something of this magnitude deserved a celebration every bit as grand as the event itself. So, the week before the wedding Jay rented a giant party van and we headed out to New Orleans.

As luck would have it, we discovered the annual Mardi Gras festivities were taking place the week before our wedding. My friends were ecstatic and couldn't believe their luck. The twelve of us piled in the back of that van and hit the open road. Making a weekend out of it, we'd spend the first night on Bourbon Street heading out in the morning to the casinos in Biloxi, Mississippi. What could possibly be better than taking a road trip with eleven of your closest friends? It was the best bachelor party ever.

The night before we were scheduled to leave, everyone met over at Bryan and Chris's house to hang out. After a couple of beers the natives were getting restless causing our departure time to be pushed up a few hours. I'm not sure Jay was fully aware of what he was getting himself into when he volunteered to drive. Being stuck with a bunch of drunken rednecks for five hours straight is not my idea of a good time, especially when you aren't one of them. Actually it was more like two hours because most everyone had already passed out cold by then.

One thing I found especially hilarious was Bryan and Eric both had a small case of poison ivy from a recent camping trip. Initially, Bryan broke out on his hands, but the rash spread quickly to his arms and face. He was itching like crazy the whole way to New Orleans. Granted, that may not seem particularly humorous but how Eric got infected, now that was funny. It seems he happened to come in contact with the poisonous plant while answering nature's call, kind of ironic when you think about it. Anyway, the rash was driving him insane and he spent half the trip with his hands down his pants screaming miserably. He's a very animated fellow and kept us in stitches with every outburst. It didn't help matters that Bryan had apparently rubbed his mouth before discovering the infection. Needless to say, there was the occasional comment from the peanut gallery, "Hey Bryan, how come you have a rash on your hands and Eric has one down there?" Thankfully, they were both pretty good sports about the whole thing. You know how guys can be when they get a little rowdy.

This was actually pretty mild compared to some of the stunts we'd pulled on them in the past. Remember how I mentioned Bryan's tendency to pass out early when he had one too many? Well one night he and Eric both crashed a little too soon and fell victim to our high jinx. There is now in existence a contraband photograph, showing the two of them cuddling closely on the floor. After rolling them together and tossing Eric's arm over Bryan, someone took it upon themselves to drape a blanket over top of them for more effect. It worked like a charm.

Buying your friends a twelve pack of beer: Twenty bucks; Witnessing the reaction on their faces the first time they see those pictures: Priceless.

I'll have to see if I can locate that picture and get it posted on my website sometime in the future. I'm sure Bryan would have no problem with that, but Eric may be slightly harder to convince. You see, Bryan is already happily married. Eric on the other hand, is still on the lookout for a potential mate which may very well raise an objection from him. He might argue that putting such an incriminating picture of him on the internet could hinder him in that pursuit.

But I'll probably post it anyway. As you can see, our ribbing those guys about the poison ivy incident was the least of their concerns. With friends like us to worry about, who needs enemies? And unlike their rashes that would be gone in a week or so, none of us were going anywhere. We're here for the long haul whether they like it or not.

After surviving many grueling hours on the road we finally reached our destination in the early afternoon. Checking into the hotel, some of the guys were anxious to get some shut eye before hitting Bourbon Street. Not Kevin and I, we were running on pure adrenaline. Stopping briefly to drop our bags off at the room, the two of us got a jump on the others downing three Hurricanes each before they ever woke up. This was my bachelor party after all, and sleeping just wasn't on the agenda. Besides, we only had one night in New Orleans and I wanted to enjoy every minute. So I hung out with Kevin, Eric, and Kevin's friend Johnny for most of the day. The rest of the gang met up with us later as the partying continued well into the night.

Things got a little hairy once when Kevin and I got separated from the rest of the group. Wandering aimlessly down Bourbon Street we suddenly found ourselves in uncomfortable terrain. I'd always heard the side streets were incredibly unsafe, home to many muggings and other violent crimes. They were poorly lit, providing the perfect spot for a criminal to on take advantage of a victim who'd likely be disoriented from consuming too much alcohol. But even after a couple drinks we knew better than to go down any dark alleys. Our problem arose as we drifted along, paying little attention to our surrounding environment. Engrossed in conversation, Kevin suddenly froze dead in his tracks. His face turned pale and it looked as though he'd just seen a ghost. Although there were no apparitions in sight, we did get a strange feeling of déjà vu, like somehow we'd experienced this moment before. Turning my eyes away from my brother, I scanned our surroundings in search of a clue to his strange behavior. At first glance everything seemed to be in order. The street was brightly lit and there were people everywhere, spilling out of the bars and onto the street. It wasn't until I took a closer look at the crowd that I figured out what was bothering him.

There were no women to be seen anywhere. Oh there were plenty of people wearing dresses and makeup, but half of them had a five o'clock shadow peeking out from underneath their masquerade. For a split second I knew how my father must've felt when he got flashbacks from the war. Regaining my composure, I realized instantly that we needed to get out of there fast. Apparently intrigued by my camouflage pants or perhaps Kevin's denim overalls, we seemed to be drawing attention from some of the "ladies". We ran back the other direction so fast it would've made your head spin. I'm sure if the folks from *Guinness* had been there with a stopwatch, we'd have set a land speed record of some sort. It seems there's one block on Bourbon Street that acts as a divider between the straight bars and the gay ones. The minute we crossed the line we found ourselves in no man's land (or every man's land depending on how you look at it). Luckily, we managed to make it out alive.

Besides this one little mishap, the remainder of the trip was surprising uneventful. Don't get me wrong, all the guys had a great time hanging out together again. It was the ultimate road trip. After a great night at Mardi Gras, we spent the next day in Biloxi gambling away the rest of our money at the casinos. I think Jay may have won a few bucks at the blackjack table but if so, he was the only one. Going home dead broke didn't dampen our spirits one bit. The whole ride back to Atlanta, everyone kept carrying on about how much fun they had and how they couldn't wait to do it again.

You'd think getting to spend a weekend out of town would be plenty of pre-wedding partying for anyone. Not for my friends. They wanted to celebrate my last day of freedom the night before the ceremony. So we made plans to hit the town shortly after the rehearsal dinner. Unable to join the festivities in New Orleans, John, Matt, and Neal (another cousin) got a chance to participate this time around. Shannon was fine with the idea as long as we promised not to be late to church. She's such a good sport. What more could a guy ask for? There's no doubt she had concerns about us going out the night before the wedding, but she didn't use any of her clout as the bride-to-be to get us to stay home. In fact, she actually encouraged us to enjoy ourselves one last time before she slapped the shackles on me once and for all. Knowing that sometimes its best to hold your tongue (I have my mother to thank for that), I kept my mouth shut and took her up on the offer.

Getting together all my rowdy friends, we met up at a local watering hole to start the night off properly. This bar in particular is widely known for the vagrants and other riffraff that can always be found inside. That's why a group of rednecks like us fit in so well. Fights broke out so often that it barely even caused a scene. I guess the regular patrons had become desensitized to these regular bouts of violence.

When things got heated between two young guys that night, most people hardly looked up from their pool table to see what the ruckus was about. They seemed far more concerned about making their next shot than with what was taking place across the bar. I don't think these two guys would have ever come to blows if not for Jay's help. He stood directly between them instigating the whole incident. "Did you hear what he said about your mother?" he'd say to one. Turning his attention to the other guy he'd say, "Are you going to let him talk to you like that?" I guess when you stand 6'9" and weigh over three hundred pounds you can get away with stuff like that. He toyed with those poor souls a while, playing one off the other until they finally cracked. The fight itself only lasted a second. Neither one of them really wanted to get physical but Jay's goading eventually pressured them into action.

As it turns out, Jay wasn't the only one harboring an aggressive streak that evening. The guys were ready to hit another bar but not before taking a brief pit stop at the restroom. Not everyone had to go, so a few of us waited out front while they finished their business.

That's when it happened. I'm standing outside having a great conversation when this guy comes barging out the front door, pushing his way through us to get into a waiting cab. He seemed pretty angry about something. But in no way did that give him the right to take it out on us. Bothered by such a rude display, I slammed my hands hard against the car window as he closed the taxi door. The noise must've startled him because he immediately jumped back against the seat. At this point, I was satisfied. In my mind his action got an equal and opposite reaction from me (one of Newton's laws). Order had been restored to the universe, or at least to our corner of the parking lot.

But this clown had to go and push the envelope. I mean he just couldn't leave well enough alone. Turning away from the cab, I noticed his middle finger extended in the window. This prick had the audacity to flick me a bird. So I did what any rational individual would do facing a situation like this. I flung open the taxi door and climbed in after him. That poor guy was scared half to death. His body was pressed up against the other side of the car as he screamed nervously to the cabbie, "Drive! Drive!" Fortunately, Kevin had the good sense to pull me back before the car tore out of the parking lot. Attempting to get into a fist fight the night before my wedding is not one of the best ideas I've ever had. But no rounds were exchanged so my face was still bruise free for the upcoming ceremony.

Before I knew it the day had finally arrived. Entering the church I found myself being ushered off into a small room to wait for our guests to be seated. My cousins and friends stood outside escorting the ladies into the sanctuary. Billy, still feeling miserable from the night before, took it upon himself to ask each person he greeted if they happened to have any aspirin with them he could borrow. Welcome to my world.

The ceremony itself was absolutely beautiful. Shannon, along with help from friends and family, did a remarkable job of decorating the church. Everything looked fabulous and my family had on their Sunday best. To the untrained eye, it may not have been blatantly obvious that the two people joining together in holy matrimony were of redneck descent. That all changed the moment Shannon's dad walked her toward the altar. Things were going great until the preacher asked "Who gives this woman's hand away in marriage?" Her father responded, "Her mother and I do...and that's my final answer!" The television show, "*Who wants to be a Millionaire*", was extremely popular then and he took this rare opportunity to quote the show in a memorable way. Everybody laughed out loud. Even the preacher got a kick out of his unexpected comment. But the gig was now up. Anyone who wasn't already aware I was marrying a redneck was now. Most of the guests already knew our backgrounds anyway, and if they thought this was odd behavior just wait until they saw the reception.

With so many people waiting to greet us after the ceremony, we knew there'd be little chance of eating for quite a while. That's why we stopped by McDonald's on the way to the reception site to grab a quick bite. It was about a twenty minute drive from the church, plenty of time to scarf down a burger and fries. The girl at the drive through window was visibly stunned as we pulled around to pay for the order. I guess it's not everyday she sees a bride and groom, crammed into the cab of a Ford Ranger, detouring long enough to get a Big Mac.

By the time we made it to the reception hall most of our guests had already arrived. A lot of my friends beat us there too, which explained the tapped kegs of beer. And by the looks of things, they decided to make themselves comfortable. Bryan was down to wearing nothing but slacks and a wife beater, but that paled in comparison to the attire of my own flesh and blood. Kevin managed to change out of his tuxedo into his trademark overalls, while John donned a pair of sunglasses and his military issue camouflage hat making a fashion statement of his own.

Everyone seemed to be having the time of their lives and I couldn't have been happier. This was a celebration after all. Shannon and I wanted people to kick back and enjoy spending the evening together. And that's exactly what they did. True to my heritage, we elected to have ribs catered from one of my favorite BBQ restaurants. Since this was the only aspect of the wedding that I took a real interest in, Shannon eventually caved. My friends gave me a great deal of flack regarding my food selection though I don't remember there being any leftovers. The dance floor was hopping right from the start, stopping just long enough for Kevin and two of his buddies to cut a rug line-dancing to the beat of *Footloose*. He also managed to gather a small group near the DJ stand to sing *Family Tradition* in my honor. And there was even a pool table upstairs for good measure. Things couldn't have turned out any better.

As the evening drew to a close, the time came for us to say goodbye. After making our way through a barrage of bubbles, we hopped in the cab of my pickup and prepared to head off. Only one problem, the windshield was covered in a mix of shaving cream and shoe polish making it impossible to see outside. A quick try of the wipers only caused it to smear, creating a bigger mess than we had in the first place. So naturally I hung my head outside the window and put the truck in gear.

There was no turning back now, like it or not my fate had been sealed. Shannon and I were anxious to begin our new life together. We felt scared and excited at the same time. Our lives were inextricably tied together from this day forward, neither of us knowing where this road might lead. The only thing we knew was that whatever lied before us would be tackled together, and somehow, that was more than enough. I released my foot off the brake and we headed out toward a beautiful horizon. Two rednecks united as one, for better or worse, ready to take on the world. But I can't help but wonder, would the world ever be ready for us?

Conclusion

I began this book with a question. What exactly is a redneck? And yet, after rambling on about my life for so many pages I still don't have a good answer. My only hope for discovering the truth was to explore my own life for clues. But what I've realized is that trying to define an entire culture using only broad generalizations and stereotypes can be a difficult, if not impossible task. That's because all people, even the redneck variety, are incredibly unique creatures in their own right. Each one is blessed with specific character traits setting them apart from the crowd. And besides, your family background, or where you come from, is far less important than where you're headed and who you become in the process.

It has been said that *fate* can be described as the unavoidable events that happen to you over the course of your life. *Destiny*, on the other hand, is how you choose to respond to those challenges. It seems that what happens *to* you is far less important than what happens *inside* of you. True character often takes years to develop and is seldom handed out at birth. We may well be given the seeds of greatness, but it is our responsibility to provide the environment they need to grow into their full potential.

Taking another look back through those old photographs, something began to dawn on me. Nearly every picture in all fourteen of my mothers' family albums revealed the same thing. Everybody appears to be so happy. Growing up without much money didn't seem to matter one bit. And judging by the huge smiles on our faces we couldn't have enjoyed life any more than we did back then. Even my parents, with all their struggles, looked completely lost in the moment as the camera froze our memories forever. Part of me wanted to reach into those old pictures and touch the past, but it just seemed to slip right through my fingers. Those days are gone and are never coming back. That's when I realized how fast life is moving. Here I am at twenty nine years old, wondering where all the time has gone. Man, I can still remember when thirty seemed so old. Now it's just around the corner and life seems to keep accelerating. Mom says it's even worse for her.

Many years of my life were spent denying my redneck roots, but today I feel especially privileged to have been part of such a wonderful family. It took me a long time to understand the value of all the wonderful gifts I'd been given. It's like the fabled tale known as *Acres of Diamonds*. In case you aren't familiar with the story, it's about a man who traveled the globe in search of great treasure only to die broke and miserable. Ironically, after his death the biggest diamond mine in the world was discovered in his own back yard. He traveled the world over looking for treasure that was right under his nose. He simply had to tap the mine. This story serves as a strong reminder to me of the many great things that have already been placed in my life. The challenge is to open my eyes wide enough to be able to see what has been there all along.

Take this book for example. There are some people I know who are under the false impression that the challenging circumstances of my life have put me at a tremendous disadvantage. That somehow my background as a redneck would have a direct and lasting impact on how successful I would eventually become. And for a while, I was in total agreement. What did it matter if I didn't succeed, it wasn't like I'd be falling short of anyone's expectations. Coming from a long line of rednecks didn't set the highest standards for achievement if you know what I mean. But now I realize that other people's opinions should never dictate a man's fate. Or a woman's either. What does matter, in fact the only thing that really matters, is what you believe deep down in your soul. People will always have their opinions. What they should know is that without the life story, *The Redneck Chronicles* would've never existed. No inspiration, no funny stories to share, and definitely no manuscript could've ever been written without first having lived through those very experiences. It's a simple matter of perspective.

But don't be jealous of me because of my roots. Go back and check your own family tree. You just might hit pay dirt and discover a redneck gene or two lying dormant somewhere in the lineage. It's quite possible that with enough digging you could strike gold too. Besides, even if you aren't able to find your link to redneck genealogy at first, don't despair. Purebreds aren't the only ones with access to our wonderful community. We happily accept converts as well, welcoming each one of you with open arms. And believe me, membership has its privileges. So remember, count your blessings, pray for divine intervention, and maybe, just maybe, one day you too will be lucky enough to call yourself a redneck.

Author's Note

If you enjoyed reading this book, you're going to love my website. I've invested plenty of sweat equity attempting to provide you, the reader, with a fantastic online experience.

Available on the website (www.brentbasham.com)

- Outrageous family photos (including many from the introduction)

- Free electronic version of the book to share with family and friends

- "Redneck of the Month" competition

- Opportunity to share your own redneck story and compete for prizes

- Email newsletter (also free) including site updates and contest winners

- Decorative photo prints from the family album

- Exclusive "Redneck Chronicles" apparel

- Hilarious slide show, "If rednecks were in charge…"

…with more coming soon. When you visit, feel free to contribute any ideas you may have to make the website experience better. And for those of you who've discovered a little bit of redneck in your own blood…

Welcome to the family!

0-595-30899-6